S

Sudeep Nagarkar has authored eleven bestselling novels: *Few Things Left Unsaid, That's the Way We Met, It Started With a Friend Request, Sorry You're Not My Type, You're the Password to My Life, You're Trending in My Dreams, She Swiped Right Into My Heart, All Rights Reserved for You, Our Story Needs No Filter, She Friend Zoned My Love* and *The Secrets We Keep*. He has been featured on the Forbes longlist of the most influential celebrities for two consecutive years. He was also awarded the 'Celebrity author of 2013' by Amazon and, in 2016, he was awarded the 'Youth Icon of the Year' by Zee Awards and WBR group.

He has given guest lectures at various organisations and institutes, including TEDx and the IITs.

Connect with Sudeep via:

Instagram: sudeepnagarkar
Facebook Fan page: facebook.com/sudeepnagarkar
Facebook Profile: facebook.com/nagarkarsudeep
Twitter: sudeep_nagarkar

# STAND BY ME!

Sudeep Nagarkar

First published by Westland Publications Private Limited in 2019

1st Floor, A Block, East Wing, Plot No. 40, SP Infocity, Dr MGR Salai, Perungudi, Kandanchavadi, Chennai 600096

Westland and the Westland logo are the trademarks of Westland Publications Private Limited, or its affiliates.

Copyright © Sudeep Nagarkar, 2019

ISBN: 9789388754736

10 9 8 7 6 5 4 3 2 1

This is a work of fiction. Names, characters, organisations, places, events and incidents are either products of the author's imagination or used fictitiously.

Typeset by SÜRYA, New Delhi

Printed at Manipal Technologies Limited, Manipal

# prologue

You think you are the creator of your own life, don't you? As if you know your ultimate motive to survive. Every step and every decision in your life is calculated to seek appreciation or benefits. But sometimes you forget that you are just a character in my story and that I decide your fate. I can screw your calculations at any given point of time. Therefore you need to trust me, the one who's writing your story. However, my advice to you is this: never, ever trust me if you are programmed to follow your intellect. Because, they say, when you trust your soul, you are often betrayed by your fate.

They say easing grief is all about putting in the mental effort, but that's like killing my very existence. When you lose the ones you love, does your mental effort give you any relief? Do you find composure in your thoughts? If I restrain you from even thinking, your efforts will be fruitless. Sometimes I have to give you a reality check, show you that I exist; I hover stealthily in an invisible silence, in a wordless voice, spending a lifetime longing to be known and heard. Your mind is your demon; it doesn't know that you can't be who you desire to be. However, I *know you won't believe that. You are a coward, all human beings are. The greed in you kills me every single day; the dissatisfaction in you and the inability to be happy in your present makes me feel useless. So I say, your mind is your demon. But I'll make you believe in me. I'll make you believe that if the universe plans to take something away from you, it has already planned to give something equally precious to you.*

*What can be will only come to be when time allows the means to seek it out. It will happen when you believe in my power. I'll make sure that happens. When the strength of your mind diminishes, the power in me only rises. You crave to make reality your own, but you forget that I am your reality, that I own it. If you don't keep faith in me, I'll change your fate and the prince of darkness in me will destroy your existence. And if you do keep faith, I'd still change your fate and the divine power will bring only smiles. The light may touch your surface but the sun won't rise if I decide against it. Remember: the cerebrum dies with you; but I, your soul, am immortal.*

## chapter one

30 November 2018

Winter mornings aren't filled with noise in Gurgaon's C Block. Yet, no one in B-12 heard the doorbell, which had rung umpteen times since sunrise.

'I'll be as free as a bird from now on; no worries, no tensions, nothing.'

Kartik work up with a jerk. The words echoed in his head, which was throbbing painfully, so much so, that he couldn't recall whether they had been voiced by a man or a woman. Rubbing his face with his large hands to coax himself awake, he sat up on his bed with a sore neck, probably from sleeping wrong.

'I'm in my room; how the hell did I get here?' he thought to himself. He still couldn't recollect who had said, 'I'll be free as a bird…' He tried to remember the events of last night—the party had continued till the wee hours—but he only had a vague memory of someone taking him to his bedroom. He did remember calling his dad, who lived in Delhi with his second wife—Kartik's stepmother—whom he disliked to the core. He had no memory of why he had called, though. The rest was a blur, and frustrated with his hangover, he finally stopped trying to remember anything. Glancing at his mobile screen, he wasn't surprised to see numerous missed calls and messages. Most of them were from those who had been at last night's party.

'Dude, it was one hell of a party; didn't have the strength to even message you after reaching home safely. The hangover is getting on my nerves now. By the way, I tried calling you and Ruhi many times since morning, I am sure you two haven't started your day yet.'

He was reading the first unread WhatsApp chat message from Mihir, his best friend for half a decade, and Ruhi's boyfriend of just over a couple of years. The call list displayed more than a dozen missed calls from him since early morning. Kartik wondered how Mihir had managed to get up so early, and then remembered through his headache that it was Ruhi's birthday.

'Please tell Ruhi to call me once she gets up. She isn't answering my calls.' This one was from Pooja, Ruhi's BFF.

*Shit, what time is it?* Kartik frantically looked at the time on his phone and saw that it was almost one in the afternoon. He had promised Ruhi a Sunday brunch and had even booked a special birthday cake at the Radisson. He stepped out of his bed and looked down at his PJs, silently thanking his drunk self for changing out of his tight jeans. After taking a shower, he walked into the kitchen. The growing headache and the dehydration made him want to eat something. There were half-eaten pizzas on the kitchen counter; glasses and empty cold-drink bottles were strewn all over the room. Then he saw the bowl full of fruit. Ruhi always made it a point to cut some for him before going to sleep when they had such parties. She had remembered to do that even last night, knowing that Kartik would crave fruits in the morning. Putting the bowl on the dining table, he went towards her room to wake her up. Before he could knock, his phone beeped. It was Dipika, their elder sister.

'Where the hell are you guys? Nobody is picking up my calls since morning.' Dipika was speaking at the top of her voice.

'Don't get mad. I already have a ton of unread messages hinting the same.' Kartik said, irritated.

'Why did you call Dad last night?' Dipika said. She sounded anxious.

'He called you?'

'Yes, he did.'

'What did he say? I don't remember the interaction we had. I was dead drunk.'

'You don't remember? You are freaking me out!'

'No, seriously, I don't. Please tell me.'

'Forget it. Is Ruhi still sleeping? Weren't you supposed to take her out for brunch?'

A brief pause followed Dipika's question. Kartik had a slight smile on his face.

'You should have been here. We missed you last night. On her last birthday, we had all gone for lunch together. Remember?'

'Of course. If I had a choice, I would have surely come. Who wants to work, especially when it's my darling little sister's birthday? Anyway, next weekend we'll be together and we'll have fun.'

'Yeah,' Kartik said, knocking on Ruhi's bedroom door.

'Okay then. Call me once you both reach Radisson.'

Dipika hung up. Kartik knocked on the door again, but there was no response. As far as he could remember, Ruhi hadn't intended to go out in the morning. She must be in her room; maybe too hungover to get up, he thought.

'Ruhi, are you there? Get up! Aren't we going for brunch?' he shouted, standing near the door.

After a few more knocks and shouts, the silence began to worry him. Was she okay? What had happened last night? Had she left with Mihir? Had she told him about going somewhere? His head just kept throbbing. Eventually, he stopped knocking, and then, after a few attempts, broke down the door.

There she was, lying on the floor, the warmth of life stolen by the cold embrace of death.

Kartik looked desperately for a flicker of life but was met with a cold stillness, broken only by the curtains fluttering in a gently blowing breeze. The clock kept on ticking, but for him, time had stopped. He gazed at her as she lay there, soulless—her words, her expressions, her smile, everything was still vivid in his memory. He didn't know how many minutes passed by; he wanted to stay there for a long time. His brain had stopped functioning. Kartik's sister was gone, stolen from him forever.

## chapter two

*Seven months later*

Pain is terrifying, but numbness is worse. That night in November, not one but two people had died. One soul escaped forever, but the other was dying every day. Kartik curled further into a messy ball as the days passed; the voices within him wouldn't allow him to live a normal life after Ruhi's death. Thoughts consumed him, and he couldn't find a way to run away from them. He just couldn't accept what had happened; it festered inside him, the person he was, the person he had become and the person he was becoming. It wasn't his fault: he went for walks, he tried to spend time with friends, but nothing worked, not even Dipika's best efforts to help him recover. There was no fixing his depression. Making him pop pills or stabbing him with needles didn't seem to help him. When the will to live deserted him a month after his sister's death, he had to be admitted to a psychiatric hospital. Doctors were trying their best to cure him, but deep inside, Kartik knew the reason he had turned silent. More than her death, what was killing him was the fact that no one believed his story. If it was just the police or other random people, he would probably have been fine. But even Dipika and his family didn't seem to trust him anymore; it had been almost seven months now that he had to live with a lie only he knew.

'Good evening, Kartik. How are you today?' Dr Rakesh Singh asked as he entered the room.

On Fridays, Kartik had one-to-one sessions with the doctor so the latter could keep tabs on his progress. Today was his twenty-fifth session and, according to Dr Singh, he was improving.

Kartik had no real answer to Dr Singh's question. What was he supposed to say? Was he supposed to blurt out that he still felt the presence of a black hole inside his mind, or that he wanted to kill himself every day? Of course, he couldn't express those feelings as they would only cage him for a few more months.

'Will saying that I am feeling better get me out of this shit?'

'It's my job to ask,' Dr Singh said with a smile as he flipped through the papers in his file. 'You know that we have to reach the root of your emotional pain, not only for the sake of our study but as a step towards healing for you. In most cases, traumatic events cause our mind to shut down; that's how our brain reacts. But I see that you have improved a lot, and if you cooperate with us, you'll soon be discharged. But remember—'

'No drinks, no drugs, no nonsense addictions, right? I have been hearing this since our first session.'

'You got my point. They only intensify your trauma, and your mind needs stability right now.'

Kartik nodded. He hated attending these sessions, but the fact was that, expressing his feelings to Dr Singh had actually helped him. Most of their conversations were about coping, but whenever Dr Singh had talked about the incident, he could feel an anger burning inside him, which scared him. During the initial sessions, when he had sat blank-faced and hardly uttered a word, Dr Singh had tried to just bring him back to life. Dipika never spoke about the incident when she visited, and the doctors had tried to spare him the recollection of those memories as well. It was only in the past few sessions that Dr Singh had talked about it; maybe they felt now that he was managing pretty well. However, Kartik cooperated only because he wanted to escape the trap. He didn't want to go back to the house for obvious reasons, but he didn't want to stay in the hospital either.

'So, how many kilometres did you cover today during your morning run?' Dr Singh continued throwing questions at him.

'Almost four. I've been timing myself with the watch given to us.' Kartik folded his hands in his lap.

'That is indeed good. The doctors were right,' Dr Singh added.

'About what?'

'That, considering the way you have kept up with the routine therapy, you'll get a discharge soon.'

The words didn't affect him. Dr Singh is just bluffing as usual to make me feel better, he thought. He looked at the doctor with a straight face and fiddled with the rosters on the table.

'Can I ask you something?' Kartik asked, after a brief pause.

'Sure. Go ahead.'

'Why are we made to run? I mean, we aren't competing in the Olympics for sure. So how does it help?'

'Running not only helps people vent their frustrations, but also helps them gain mental composure.'

Kartik didn't believe the latter was true, but he knew that it did help with the frustration and the anger. In fact, he had made it a habit to run as fast as he could before the sessions to keep his head cool.

'I don't know how you'll take this, but I think I have to tell you.' Dr Singh looked straight into his eyes as if he was trying to hypnotise him. Before Kartik could respond, he continued, 'The police want to meet you tomorrow morning. I have to agree to this; I know you hate talking to them, and maybe you want to hit me with those rosters, but I have no choice.'

'Why do they have to meet me now? They closed the case. Didn't they?'

'Maybe a closing formality? I have told them not to be too harsh with you.'

'They don't believe anything I say, anyway,' Kartik said angrily. He didn't want to talk to the cops. It was useless and made him feel depressed, for they had been rejecting the story he had narrated from the very first day. Besides, the more they questioned him, the more he felt like a loser for not being able to remember anything about that night.

He wanted to run away that very moment—somewhere no one knew him, and no one would keep him like a caged bird. He wanted to bang his head on a wall in sheer helplessness.

*I have to resist, this can't be happening. Why are they after my life? In any case they think I am an alcoholic, that my story is fake, and my statement can't be considered because my mental health is fucked up. So how the fuck do these meetings help? Let them go ahead with their stupid fabricated story. Close the case once and for all, terming it as suicide.*

'The case is closed! What do they want from me now? Can't I just be allowed to live a normal life? I have lost Ruhi forever; Dipika is all alone outside while I am in a goddamn fucking cage here. Why can't they just leave us be?'

'Trust me, Kartik. Everything will be okay,' Dr Singh reassured him, and he realised he would have to go along.

*How much more helpless can a person get? Just so I can leave this bloody place and show that I am all right, I have to agree with the doctors, talk to the police. I wish I could have died instead of Ruhi; this life is worse than death. Why did you leave us, Ruhi? Why? We loved you, we did.*

*You were everything to us. I just can't stand this loss. Please come back, for my sake!*

~

'Kartik Sharma, how are you feeling now?' Inspector Kumawat asked. He paced the room a couple of times before he sat down on the black chair opposite Kartik. He was the same police officer who had come to the house on the morning after the incident.

*Dead*, Kartik said in his mind, but replied, 'Better.' The conversation was being recorded, and he didn't want to give the doctors a chance to think otherwise.

*Why is this happening to me? Why am I stuck in this mess?*

Kartik's fingernails bit into his palms, imprinting red crescents on his skin; he twiddled his thumbs, then realised that it would be interpreted as a sign of nervousness. At least he had learned that much during his stay in the hospital.

'Do you mind telling me again what happened on the night of 29 November?'

Kartik shook his head. The tears that suddenly flooded his eyes blurred his vision. He couldn't handle the horrible memories stirring in his mind, nor the guilt associated with those memories. It was as if the image of Ruhi's pale, lifeless body was imprinted on his brain. Still, he told himself to remain strong—for some reason even he couldn't fathom, because he had lost the desire to live.

'What happened on the night of 29 November, Mr Kartik?' Inspector Kumawat pressed.

Kartik shook his head again, indicating that he wasn't willing to speak about the incident. He wasn't sure what part of the ordeal was worse—living it or having to constantly recount the events to the police.

'Mr Kartik?' Inspector Kumawat was losing patience. 'Do you agree with the version of events recorded in the police report?'

Silence greeted Inspector Kumawat's question. Kartik's mind had flittered elsewhere. More specifically, to the darkest morning of his life. His fingernails cut deeper into his palms, bringing him back to reality.

'No, I do not agree with that version. It is not the truth. You simply want to close the case and have found an escape route by declaring it a suicide. Ruhi didn't kill herself.' Kartik was furious.

'So you still believe in the statement you gave at that time?' Inspector Kumawat looked into the file he was holding.

'Of course. But how does it matter now? Why are you bringing this up all of a sudden when your department has already closed the case?' Kartik blurted out in anger.

'We are just cross-checking all the open files to seal them permanently. It's routine procedure,' Inspector Kumawat replied matter-of-factly, adding, 'So you think the stalker you saw outside the apartment that evening had been chasing Ruhi for quite some time? And he broke into your house after the party and killed her?'

'I believe you've already recorded my statement. Haven't you?' Kartik was getting increasingly irritated with the entire discussion which, he knew, would yield nothing.

'You still have to repeat it for the final recording.'

Kartik remembered what Dr Singh had said last night. *'Trust me, everything will be okay.'* Replaying the words in his mind, he tried to compose himself to give his statement once again, hoping it would be the last time he would have to repeat it.

'Yes, it was him. I had seen him a few times before, and a couple of times on the evening of the 29th. The first time I saw him that evening, Ruhi was arguing with him. He had his back to me, so it didn't immediately strike me that he was the same guy who had been hovering around our apartment. He had this long ponytail and was wearing a white shirt.'

'And you have said that, after the argument with your sister, you saw him again later that night outside your apartment?'

'Yes. The party was about to start when I saw a guy—same appearance, white shirt and ponytail—and realised he was the one I'd often spotted hanging around our apartment, sometimes glancing towards our bedroom windows. Then I realised he was the one I'd seen with Ruhi earlier in the evening. I wish I could've stabbed him then and there. I still feel responsible for her death. I still feel he was the one who came out of her room that night and took me to my bedroom. Maybe he was the one who said, "I'll be as free as a bird from now on; no worries, no tensions, nothing".'

'But you've said in your statements so far that you weren't sure who that was. So, are you sure now? Also why didn't you ask her about him that night, if not in the evening when you saw her with the man?' Inspector Kumawat asked.

'I've already told you, I didn't want to spoil her party. I was planning to talk to her about it the next day. I am not sure if he is the one who took me to my bedroom, but I am certain that he killed Ruhi. He is the one who added all those sedatives to her last drink, which caused her death.' The guilt was evident in Kartik's voice.

'But why would she accept a drink offered by a stalker? That too, after everyone had left, including her boyfriend, Mihir.'

'I don't know; it was your job to find out.'

'How many drinks did you have that night?'

'I don't remember.' Kartik didn't even want to remember.

'That says it all, Mr Kartik. We just can't go ahead with your statement. Neither then, nor now. No matter what you think, you have to trust us. The stalker never existed. He never entered your apartment—the security guard has no record of a visitor coming to your apartment after midnight. Once the party was over, Ruhi killed herself. The sooner you accept the fact, the better it will be for you,' Inspector Kumawat said, stamping his verdict on the case, once and for all.

'Fine, whatever,' Kartik said and took a deep breath. He was done with all of it. No one believed him. According to the cops, it was a suicide. But he believed that his sister was murdered. The truth, however, had been silenced, along with Ruhi.

~

Having a sister is a blessing, and Kartik was truly blessed to have two: one who looked after him as a mother would have, and one who lived with him as a friend. Dipika was the eldest of the three, and Ruhi the youngest. In a world where we often hear stories of fights and grudges between brothers and sisters in dysfunctional families, these three were the epitome of sibling love.

No matter how much they argued, Ruhi and Kartik were inseparable. For Kartik, Ruhi had been a joy and comfort since the day she was born. She was the friend who helped him through difficult times; her consoling words were worth more to him than all the wealth in the world. He was always a little reserved in Dipika's presence, as she was the eldest. But Ruhi was his partner-in-crime, a companion to whom he could express his feelings.

Being the youngest in the family has advantages of its own. You are certainly ordered to do all the little chores at home, but on special occasions, you are totally pampered. And it was no different for Ruhi. 29 November was Ruhi's day, the eve of her twenty-fifth birthday. Kartik had organised a surprise party for her that night, followed by a special outing the next day, but pretended that he had absolutely no plans. He went to work that morning like it was any other day, but as he drove back, his car was crammed with all the party stuff, including the booze and decorations. He had written a special note for Ruhi and pasted it on his gift for her, which was now in the car's passenger seat. While he waited at a red light with music playing on his stereo, he glanced at the note to read it again:

*Never can it be said that there is a better sister in this world than you. You are amazing in every way. I'd rather have you than a thousand friends beside me. Looking forward to many more late-night talks and shopping days with you. Here's a surprise for you this year, and for many more. Happy birthday, my little sister.*

It brought a smile to his face. He loved and cared for his sister unconditionally. After moving out of their parent's house, he felt she was his responsibility, and a special, inseparable bond had developed between the siblings.

He called Ruhi to inform her that he had left office early and was on his way home.

'Are you home?' he asked.

'No bhai, I am at the supermarket for some groceries. Why?'

'Nothing special. I'm coming home early, so I thought I would check and see if you're there.'

'Okay. By the way, Dipika called to say she can definitely make it for brunch tomorrow,' Ruhi said.

'Are you sure? That's great! Anyway, I'll see you soon. I'll reach in fifteen,' Kartik said and hung up.

The news about Dipika delighted him, as he had thought she would be missing out on brunch the next day. They had followed this tradition on Ruhi's birthday for the past few years, but Dipika had said she would have to stay over at the office for a late-night meeting, and might have to miss the brunch for the first time. Kartik thought of calling Dipika right then, but just as he entered the lane of their apartment building, he saw Ruhi near the park that faced the main gate of the colony. He was puzzled—she had said she was at the supermarket just a few minutes ago. He thought of calling out to her, but dropped the idea when he saw that she was talking to someone. It seemed as if they were arguing about something. The guy had his back towards Kartik, and the lane was too dark for him to see anything clearly, but the long ponytail and white shirt couldn't go unnoticed. He certainly wasn't Mihir, Ruhi's boyfriend.

*Why did she lie to me? Who is this guy, and what is he doing here at this time? Should I just go and check, maybe ask her directly what is happening? He could be a friend, but judging from her gestures, this is no regular argument. And if he's a friend, then why did she lie about meeting him? There certainly aren't any grocery bags in her hand.*

These thoughts hammered through his head, and when he had almost decided to get out of the car and cross the lane to go towards them, the guy started walking away. Ruhi crossed the road to Kartik's side, but didn't see his car parked at the end of the lane. Kartik was in two minds; he wanted to ask Ruhi about what was happening that very moment, but he feared that it would upset her and spoil the party for her. Seven months later, in his hospital room, he wished he had decided otherwise. Even today, he was clueless as to who that person was and what his intentions had been. Sometimes, he even felt like the police were right after all—that the man had never existed. But no, he *had* seen him that day, not once but twice. As far as Kartik was concerned, that man surely did exist. He wished he could alter that night—if not delete it completely from the calendar. Some decisions can turn your entire life upside down, and not talking to Ruhi about what he had seen that evening had certainly changed Kartik's.

## chapter three

*Why would the stalker, if that is what he was, go so far as to murder Ruhi?* Kartik was too wrapped up in this thought to notice that Dr Singh had entered the room where they had their weekly sessions. This wasn't the day they usually had their meeting, however, and Kartik was unsure why a session had been scheduled overnight.

Dr Singh took his seat and silently looked at Kartik. That frustrated Kartik to no end—the doctor sitting right in front of him, observing him without saying a word.

Kartik had to break the silence. 'What's happening? Don't tell me I have to go over it all, again…?'

'What's on your mind, Kartik?' It was like the man knew exactly what he was thinking, because he didn't even flinch at his sudden outburst.

'Nothing. What do you want to know?' Kartik preferred not to speak his mind after what had happened the previous day with the cops.

'I want to hear it all today. I know there's a volcano of thoughts inside you, and I want it to erupt. Remember,

I told you that getting to the root of the emotional trauma is the key to coping with it, and an important step in the therapy. We just can't run from it.'

'I am not running away from it. I just don't want to recall it.'

'That's as good as running away from it. I want to know what happened that night. Do you think you could try telling me? I think it's the right time.'

'No, not again. I have said it all.'

'I don't think so. You have told me what you think happened. I want to know exactly how you felt. There's a difference between the two. Will you try talking about it?'

Kartik dug his nails into his palms again. Somehow, that seemed to calm him down. He stared at the papers stacked on the table in front of him and shook his head.

'I know it's difficult. Today's might be the most difficult session for you ... that's why I wanted it to be impromptu. Giving you time to prepare may have increased your anxiety.'

Kartik looked into Dr Singh's eyes, trying to gauge why he was doing all this. But somewhere deep inside, it felt good to be asked how exactly he'd felt that night. How exactly he felt now.

'Before we talk about that night, I would like to know more about your family. Maybe you could start by telling me about your relationship with your sisters and your equation with your parents ... what the dynamics are? Will that relax you a bit?'

Another useless session, Kartik thought. He couldn't comprehend how any conversation that would end in the events of that night could make him feel better. Still, as always, he gave in. He pushed hard to find composure within; it wasn't easy for him anymore. He took a few deep breaths and drifted back to the time when he, Dipika, Ruhi and their father lived under one roof, along with their stepmother.

~

Imagine a life in which your mother breathes her last when you are barely a teenager. Within a couple of years, your dad remarries and lets you know that you have to treat a complete stranger as your mother. It's torture, especially when that woman doesn't want you in your dad's life. As a child, what choice do you have? People often cry over the little worries they face in their daily life, forgetting that their family stands rock-solid beside them. For us, little worries hardly mattered; we just hoped for a normal family life. Sadly, that never happened. My dad loved me and my sisters deeply, but we could see that woman's influence on him grow by the day. Initially, she seemed tolerable, but in our final months at home, they fought constantly. My stepmother never loved us or showed an iota of motherly care. So we never treated her as our mother. Dad was always trying to break the ice between us; but, it never happened. Ideally, in a situation like this, a father would choose his children's happiness over that of a second wife who was determined to dominate us and to break our happy family apart. Instead, my dad tried to compromise and, one day, our life had to shatter.

'Can't you just leave them somewhere? What life are we living? I didn't marry you just to take care of them,' my stepmother was yelling in the hallway. She continued, 'I have my own life and I want to spend it with you; just you and me spending quality time with no interference from these idiots.'

I hated holidays because of the constant fighting. My first-year exams were going on, but who cared? By then, I didn't even bother to go out when the daily drama began. Dipika was watching television; her MBA exams had just ended. I was reading a novel, sitting on the adjoining bed. Their voices were loud and clear; it wouldn't have surprised us if the neighbours filed a complaint with the police.

'For god's sake, can we stop fighting over this? Didn't you know that I had three children when we got married? You knew it, and even promised to take care of them. Now why are you creating a fuss? It's still you and me; we do spend quality time, but you crib all the time. It's affecting their studies, these fights are affecting my work, and the entire family is getting disturbed. Why don't you understand?' my dad retaliated.

'Family? You call this a family? I am sorry, Pravin, but this is not happening. You have to take a decision today. It's enough now.'

The argument continued even when the door opened and Ruhi walked in, welcomed by yet another pleasant scene. She barged into our room and threw down her bag.

'I don't get it, I just don't get it. Why can't they stop arguing? They are always bickering with each other over us,' she yelled, and walked into the kitchen. 'I'm so sick and tired of always hearing the same thing,' she said and slammed a glass down on the marble counter. 'Why can't we just have normal parents? Why?'

'Calm down, Ruhi,' Dipika said. She went up to her and held her by her shoulders to try and console her.

'I just needed to go somewhere, anywhere but here … my own house,' she said, before retreating into our bedroom again. I was still reading a book, trying to ignore all the drama in the house.

Ruhi continued, 'I mean, they never stop. They're at each other's throats all the time. Why did they have to marry in the first place? The way they act, they should've been divorced long ago.'

Dipika sat down beside Ruhi, placed an arm around her shoulders, and looked at her wide-eyed.

'What?'

'You just need to calm down. No matter what happens, we three should always be each other's strength,' Dipika said, snatching the book from my hand to involve me in the conversation.

'What did I do? She's a bitch. Why bother stressing ourselves for no reason, because of her. I wish Mom was alive.'

'That's true. I am just so tired of it,' Ruhi cried, beginning her rant again.

'How about we watch your favourite movie again to get your mind off things?' Dipika suggested, walking over and switching the TV to smart mode.

'No, I just can't watch *Life of Pi* right now. Not a movie about a boy who cares about animals. Here, our dad doesn't even care about his children.'

Dipika walked back over to us as the previews started. She placed an arm around each of us and said, 'Just shut up and watch.'

Ruhi couldn't help but melt. Dipika always knew how to make both Ruhi and me feel better, no matter how bad things were. She always said, 'If there wasn't anything, there wouldn't be anything.' It sounded pretty simple, but it was actually a deep and complicated thought. She meant that if I wasn't her brother, she wouldn't be a sister. That part of who she is, is because of Ruhi and me. One thing we three had realised since the trouble began was that we were inseparable.

Halfway through the movie, when the doorbell rang, we knew it was our pizza delivery boy. Dipika always ordered a pizza when we watched a movie together, and we were so used to it that it wasn't a surprise anymore. However, that day, the surprise was that Dad came into the room to hand the pizza to us. It wasn't that he hadn't done it before. He knew Ruhi loved pizza, and every time he bought us one, he had that excited, broad smile on his face. But this time, he was expressionless.

We knew something wasn't right. We feared his silence, even though we knew what it meant. It was inevitable, and yet we had hoped that it would never happen. Our father had been successfully manipulated into turning his back on us. That woman was a curse on our family. If there was no law against it, she wouldn't have thought twice before killing us. Deep in my heart, I still feel she should never have come into Dad's life, our lives. I think of my mom, somewhere in this universe, full of regrets for having left us fragile and vulnerable.

~

'So, he did turn his back on you?' Dr Singh asked, taking a sip of water from the glass on his table.

Kartik stared at the glass of water, blank-faced. Then a tear rolled down his cheek and Dr Singh saw it. 'Are you okay? If you wish, we can stop here. I don't want you to be uncomfortable or stressed.'

'No, it's fine.' Kartik wiped away his tears roughly and took a deep breath. 'The bond that had held all of us together for so long broke that day.' Dr Singh folded his arms across his chest as Kartik continued. 'He had to take a decision; it was forced on him. Somehow, I had thought he would choose us, but I was wrong. We were all wrong. He came to us with the pizza and told us that he had decided to shift us to our college hostels. Our stepmother not only wanted to separate us from our dad, but from each other as well, and that wasn't acceptable. We refused. Eventually, he asked us to move to our other apartment in C Block, Sector 9, Gurgaon. We had no choice.'

'So how did you guys manage the finances, staying by yourself?' Dr Singh asked. He seemed genuinely curious.

Kartik glanced everywhere but at Dr Singh. He didn't even try to hide his nervousness. How could he when everything about this session was making him anxious. After a brief pause, he willed himself to answer Dr Singh's question. *The finances.*

'Dad is well off. He transferred money to Dipika's account every month, saying it was his responsibility. In the beginning, he even spent time with us, visiting us once or twice a week. But as the years passed, he only occasionally kept track of our whereabouts. Soon we realised that we were just a liability for him.'

The only positive aspect of those years was the way Kartik, Ruhi and Dipika stood by each other through thick and thin. Whether it was hanging out and having fun or taking charge of household chores, they had done it all together.

'And it continues even now? The financial support?'

With every question Dr Singh asked, Kartik was getting more and more emotional, thinking of what they'd had to go through.

'Once Dipika and I started working, we told him not to do us any more favours. We were okay with letting him go, so he could live his life, but Ruhi never forgave him.'

'And why do you say that?'

Kartik sighed. Moments from Ruhi's birthday a couple of years back flashed through his mind. Memories are like fire. They can inspire us or burn us like nothing else can. Looking back at the smiles that he had shared with his loved ones, Kartik found comfort within his discomfort even in that moment.

~

*I would have taken the easy path*
*But that would leave no room for glory.*
*I would have picked out a comfortable life*
*But that isn't God's kind of story.*

These words from the Alyssa Underwood poem *The Life Chosen for Me* were pinned on Kartik's work desk. After shifting to their new home in Gurgaon, these words had given him the strength to look ahead in life. Kartik and his sisters became accustomed to their new lifestyle within a few months. Being at home had never given them the joy they shared in their new life. They created their own rituals of togetherness, which they couldn't have done back home. If it was a sibling's birthday, one of the others would take them out for brunch. No matter how tight their schedules were, every other commitment was set aside as they believed in celebrating special moments together. They knew how cruel life could get. So why not collect memories and make new stories? In time, that would be the only true wealth they were left with.

'Ruhi, make it quick. We are already late. I hope they won't cancel our booking,' Dipika shouted as she shoved her phone into her purse, all set for Ruhi's birthday brunch. She had booked a table at the Radisson, like she did every year. Ruhi's birthdays were all the more special as both Dipika and Kartik treated their youngest sibling as no less than a princess.

'It's my birthdayyyyy!' Ruhi screamed from inside her room, as she adjusted her brand new birthday dress. She had a couple more, but had selected the one she was wearing after trying on the other two.

'I wish I could buy some patience from her. I get bored even taking a shower on my birthday, and here she is, changing one outfit after other,' Kartik commented. He was still in his shorts, knowing Ruhi would take at least half an hour more.

'You'll only use that patience to not move your butt from the sofa while watching some web series,' Dipika said with a smirk.

'You know me well, don't you?'

'Get lost and change your clothes, for God's sake,' Dipika said and threw a napkin at him.

Kartik got up lazily, picking up his t-shirt and jeans, but hung around waiting for Ruhi to come out from her room. And there she was, looking gorgeous in her pink dress. The glow on her face reflected her happiness. Seeing her happy and excited brought smiles to Dipika and Kartik's faces. They shared a special bond that was impossible to describe; it could only be felt and understood by the siblings themselves. Whatever the world had in store for them, they knew they would never give up on each other.

'We both want to tell you something. We don't know how you'll react, but we have to,' Dipika said once they had settled down at their table at the Radisson. She and Ruhi looked steadily at Kartik, who was sitting across the table from them.

'I am getting a bad feeling. Don't tell me you both are...' Kartik said and smirked.

'Cut the crap. Look, we haven't kept any secrets from each other, and yesterday, when Ruhi told me she had met someone special, I thought even I should confess, and we had this long heart-to-heart session,' Dipika said.

'So you both are already done with your girl talk, and now you're telling me as we're about to invite guests for the wedding.'

'We are planning a get-together,' Ruhi informed him.

'And what am I supposed to do there? You will be with your boyfriend and she will be with hers. I don't have a girlfriend to introduce. Should I just look at this as a training session from your boyfriends on how to date a girl?' Kartik said, showing his disinterest. 'Also, I'm a little upset that you didn't include me in your talk yesterday. Were you waiting for me to sleep?'

'Yes,' Ruhi said, grinning.

Kartik rolled his eyes at her teasing, and just when they were beginning to enjoy their brunch, their father called. At first, Ruhi wanted to cut the call—his voice only reminded her of all the unhappy times in the past—but Dipika saw his name on the phone and insisted that she pick up.

'He must be calling to wish you. Don't ignore it. Get it over with.'

'Why does he even call? He knows I hate him,' Ruhi said. She made a face and finally answered the call.

After the initial greetings and birthday wishes, the irritation on Ruhi's face was evident. She clearly just wanted to hang up on him. Eventually, she reached the end of her patience.

'Dad, we are out having lunch and you are disturbing us. Why do you have to interfere in our quality time? You can keep calling Kartik and Dipika on their birthdays, but please don't carry out these formalities with me. When we needed you the most, you turned your back on us, and now you think you can act like everything is normal and hope that I'll forgive you? These two will, but don't expect such things from me. Please, for heaven's sake, don't call. Sorry, but I have to go.'

Dipika and Kartik glanced at each other and then at Ruhi. They knew that it was impossible to make her understand and had given up a long time ago.

'What?' Ruhi asked, noticing that both of them were staring at her.

'What the fuck was that?' Kartik couldn't control his laughter although he sensed Ruhi's frustration.

'Can we come back to the topic we were discussing?' Dipika interrupted.

'Yeah, your boyfriends. So, when are we meeting them?'

Kartik acted as if he was curious, although he wasn't. Ruhi was quick to catch on and told him not to pretend he was interested. Finally, the plan was fixed for the coming weekend.

'In your case, I can't comment,' Kartik said, looking at Dipika. Then he turned to Ruhi and, pretending to be stern, said, 'But your guy has to first meet my approval; after all I am your elder brother.'

Dipika couldn't help but smile. She thought about the special bond the three of them shared. No stranger would believe that they were siblings and not the best of friends; such was their connection.

Kartik glanced at both Ruhi and Dipika, as thoughts of how quickly they had grown up consumed him. Both Ruhi and Kartik had been teenagers when they moved out of their dad's home. They had barely known then what life was or how to live it. They had laughed, cried and lived together ever since. Looking back, he felt blessed to be with these beautiful souls who valued his presence and made his life worth living. The years had passed by in the blink of an eye, it seemed.

~

'Kartik?' Dr Singh's voice sounded far away. 'Are you feeling better?'

Kartik's heart was beating really fast. He could remember everything like it had happened just yesterday.

Every moment was still fresh in his mind. *Why aren't there any clear pictures of that night, then? Why can't I recollect anything that happened?* There were no answers, only questions that never stopped haunting him.

'We'll continue in our next session. Now, are you feeling better?' Dr Singh repeated.

'Yes.'

## chapter four

After brunch, Dipika and Kartik headed back to their offices. Ruhi had made plans to meet Mihir. He had gone out of town on a work assignment and was supposed to come back a day later, but had just landed in Delhi to give her a surprise. Ruhi was flabbergasted when he called to tell her that he was already at Delhi airport and had taken the day off just to spend it with her.

They had known each other for a year now, and the few months they had been a couple was enough for them to realise they wanted a lifetime of togetherness. From meeting through Ruhi's brother, to following each other on Instagram to spending time together, to eventually falling in love, their story was a sure-fire bestseller. When Mihir was around, Ruhi felt safe, and wherever he was, she felt at home. He was the one person she relied on and found solace in, after Dipika and Kartik. It's been said that love is blind, but looking at them, anyone would disagree: love isn't blind; blindness is an affliction of those who have never loved.

Full of excitement, she waited for Mihir to pick her up at the Radisson, as it was on his route from the airport. Once she got into the cab with him, she couldn't hold back the news anymore.

'Guess what, I told Dipika and even Kartik that I'm in a relationship.'

'Are you serious?' It rather shocked him.

'Yes, we've even planned a get-together, along with Dipika's boyfriend.' Ruhi held his hand tight and leaned on his shoulder, as if to assure him that there wouldn't be any complications.

'Did you tell Kartik who your boyfriend is? What was his reaction?' Mihir's heart was in his mouth.

The cab moved swiftly with no traffic blocks on the roads, but Ruhi's surprise had certainly blocked the thoughts that ran through Mihir's mind. He had good reason to be anxious. He had been Kartik's best friend for quite some time. Mihir had been planning to tell Kartik that he was dating Ruhi, but every time he tried, he failed. Apprehension had always won over his faith in his friend, and even now, when Ruhi had revealed half the truth, he was panicking. Mihir knew that delaying the talk with Kartik would only complicate matters, but he still didn't feel up to it. He just couldn't anticipate what Kartik's reaction would be.

Ruhi could sense that Mihir was in a real tizzy, and said playfully, 'No, I haven't told him that yet. How about surprising him at the get-together?'

'You've gone crazy. He'll kill one of us, for sure. Shit, I'm panicking like anything,' Mihir responded, pulling his hand away from hers as he tried to compose himself.

Ruhi said nothing, only pulled him close and kissed his cheek to calm him down. She knew her brother in and out, and was sure that he wouldn't object to their relationship. She was also sure that Dipika would accept it too, as all they had ever wanted was her happiness. Now, that lay with Mihir. Her kiss soothed him a bit and they hugged for a while, without caring what the cab driver would think. That moment simply had to be sealed.

'Are we going to Ambience Mall?' Ruhi asked, seeing that the car was passing through the main gate of the mall.

'Yes, we'll first go to the bowling arcade, your favourite, and have some drinks. Then we'll watch a movie and get something to eat. That is the plan,' Mihir said.

He knew exactly what Ruhi loved to do. In the very short span of time they had spent together, he had made every effort to understand her likes and dislikes. That meant the world to Ruhi as she had met very few people in her life who genuinely cared for her. Mihir was certainly one of them.

'I love you so much.' Ruhi hugged him again, giving him a broad smile.

'I love you too.' Mihir kissed her forehead.

Once they had entered the bowling arcade and ordered their drinks, Mihir took a small box out of his bag and placed it in front of her. Ruhi was awestruck that he had remembered: she had once mentioned that she had always wanted a gold ring for a birthday gift. She couldn't believe he had actually got her one.

'You are the most amazing person I have ever met, and I want to give us a shot. Give me the best return gift I could ever ask for. Be mine?' Mihir asked, holding the ring out to her.

Ruhi retracted her hands in shock, covering her smile and bright red cheeks. She shook her head in disbelief, staring at the ring.

'Ruhi?' Mihir said so loudly that other people turned to look at them. She looked up into his irresistible puppy-dog eyes and her heart melted.

'Yes,' she whispered. 'Yes, I will.'

He placed the ring on her finger and she flung her arms around his neck, her tears soaking into his shirt. He buried his face in her hair, whispering 'I love you' over and over again.

'Thank you so much for making this birthday special. It was my first with you and I was a little nervous, but now I am content. I really love you, Mihir,' Ruhi said. Wiping her happy tears, she added, 'But I am not going to spare you from now on. On my twenty-fifth birthday, I want a diamond ring. You still have a couple of years, so start saving. I am high-maintenance, you know?' She laughed.

Though she said it jokingly, Mihir promised to give Ruhi a diamond ring on her twenty-fifth birthday. To even start describing how deeply they loved each other, one would need a thousand-page manuscript written in the most romantic idiom. Ruhi found absolute security in his embrace; his heart was her home. It was no different for Mihir. He would give up the entire world if it meant he could have her in his life forever. If love were a poem, to him 'Ruhi' would be the title.

~

'That's my birthday gift,' Ruhi sent a message on their family WhatsApp group, with a photograph in which she was flaunting her new ring. Kartik and Dipika were both on their way home from work, but responded by sending heart emojis. Ruhi put the ring in a drawer in her bedroom and went into the kitchen for a snack. Finding nothing to eat, she picked up a bottle of juice and went back to her room. Relaxing on the bed, she messaged Mihir.

*I reached home. Thank you for the wonderful day and the most precious gift. I am always going to flaunt it. And don't forget, you have to start saving for my 25th birthday gift! Love you so much. I don't know if someone else would have done all that you do for me, but now that I have you, I don't want anyone else. Be mine always.'*

After gulping down her juice, she went into the bathroom. As she turned the shower on, she thought she heard someone entering the house and bolting the door behind them.

'Dipika, is it you…?' Ruhi shouted from inside the washroom, turning the shower off so she could hear better.

No one responded, but she could hear a few noises. She was sure someone had entered the house. She called out again. 'Kartik, are you home? Who is it?'

There was no response. Frightened, Ruhi dried herself with a towel and wrapped it around her body. She double-checked that the bathroom door was locked from the inside and switched off the lights. Luckily, she had a habit of taking her phone along when she took a shower. Putting it on silent so as not to make any sound, she messaged on the siblings' WhatsApp group:

*Someone's in the house. Am hiding in the bathroom. Please come home soon. I am scared.*

Ruhi was terrified, trapped in what felt like the perfect scenario for an '80s thriller movie. She didn't want to call anyone, in case the intruder heard her speak. Forehead creased with worry, sweat running down her face and neck, she listened to the intruder stomp down the corridor that led to the other bedroom. The house was silent as death but for the sound of his movements. He must be a burglar, she thought, looking for valuables to steal. If that was true, he would find a few thousand rupees in the unlocked drawer in Kartik's bedroom. But no, she could hear the intruder retracing his steps and entering her bedroom. Ruhi suddenly had a gut feeling that he was searching for one thing and one thing only: her. She cowered behind the shower curtains as she saw the bedroom lights being switched on and off. The man was relentless. She just wished someone would arrive soon and put an end to this terror.

Dipika and Kartik had already talked on the phone about Ruhi's message. Kartik kept calling her as he drove the rest of the way, but none of his calls were picked up. He sped down the Gurgaon highway, fearing the worst. Ruhi could see her brother's calls but was too scared to pick up—the intruder would hear her voice and might try to break open the bathroom door. But her silence gave Kartik a terrible anxiety attack. *Who could it be? A thief, or someone who had gone there with the intention of hurting Ruhi?* In either case, Ruhi was in danger, and he simply had to reach home before she was harmed in any way.

But fate had other plans for Kartik. Before he could exit the highway, the cops stopped his car. He thought desperately that he would flee and pay the fine later, as time was slipping through his fingers. But they had set up a barricade across the road. Just a routine inspection, but the cops had already seen him using his mobile phone while driving well past the speed limit.

'Licence?' one of the cops asked.

Kartik handed it over and asked what the matter was.

'Did you check the speed limit while driving? Also, the department has put up huge hoardings telling you not to use your mobile while driving ... I assume you know the rules?' the cop said in a firm voice as he checked Kartik's licence and papers.

'Sir, I have to leave, please resolve this matter here. My sister is in trouble,' Kartik pleaded.

'Everyone has some urgent work lined up when caught. Don't fool around,' the cop said, unmoved by Kartik's pleas.

Agonised at the thought of what Ruhi must be going through, he tried to call her again in the midst of all the confusion. Again, the call went unanswered. By then, Dipika too wasn't picking up calls, making him even more anxious. Suddenly his phone beeped; it was a message from Ruhi.

*There's a lot of noise. I feel like I'll black out any minute now. Come soon.*

Kartik was plunged into a state of darkness where his eyes could see but the inside of his head was just pitch black. He could barely breathe, as if his thoughts were clogging his throat, blocking his airway and suffocating him from inside, crawling like little worms that were killing him very slowly. Then, out of nowhere, he heard someone calling his name.

'Kartik...'

He looked up and saw it was a young uniformed officer who had called out his name. Kartik didn't know what to say—he couldn't remember having met him before.

'What's wrong?' the officer asked, before turning to his colleague to say, 'What happened with him?'

After taking the other cop aside for a quick discussion, the officer handed Kartik's licence and papers back to him, saying, 'I am Tushar. The area in-charge officer ... and Dipika's boyfriend. I think she told you about us today, right?'

Kartik simply nodded, not knowing how to react—whether to greet him or explain the situation to him. He chose the latter as there was no time for formalities.

'Ruhi's in trouble. Someone just—'

Before he could finish, Tushar interrupted. 'She's fine. Dipika reached home just a few minutes ago and found her unconscious in the bathroom. Looks like the guy was a burglar. I have told Dipika to lodge a complaint at the local police station.'

Kartik was too overwhelmed to comprehend what was happening. Should he believe Dipika's boyfriend, who had every reason to tell him the truth and to help him, or should he simply rush home to see for himself? This time, too, he chose the latter, but not before thanking Tushar. He rushed into the house as soon as he had parked the car. Dipika was sitting beside Ruhi, who was fast asleep on her bed. He looked around—everything in the room was scattered. It was a burglar, Dipika informed him, and only some cash had been stolen, as the jewellery was inside a locker with a digital code. However, hearing the noises outside the bathroom, Ruhi had blacked out. She was all right now, Dipika added. Kartik was almost in tears as he looked down at Ruhi. He was just grateful that nothing had happened to her.

## chapter five

There are times when you feel so dejected, all you want to do is curl up into a ball and cry. There are times when you feel like the whole world is out to get you. You keep dealing with one curveball after another with everything you've got. And then, there are times when you feel like you've fallen into a black hole, a bottomless pit with no way out. But even in the darkest of times, when you feel like you've exhausted all your options and you lose all hope and think that it's all over, a ray of light appears, that leads you forward and sets you back on track. For Dipika, that ray of hope was Tushar.

When she and her siblings had shifted to Gurgaon, she was burdened with the responsibility of being the eldest in the house at an age when she had no experience in handling such a situation. She had felt it would be impossible to deal with the challenge, but then she had met Tushar after her MBA, and she had realised that life has its way of bringing you hope in the most unexpected ways. Through thick and thin, they loved each other unconditionally.

'So, I am finally meeting your family today,' Tushar said. He had picked up Dipika at the entrance to her office.

*Family.* As the word swirled around in her head, she wished it included her dad and mom. Dipika didn't hate her dad. He was barely a presence in her life now, and she had gotten over the separation a while ago. But now, with Tushar meeting her family, she realised that she wished for her dad to be a part of it. However, she was content in the belief that her mom would have been happy to meet Tushar.

'You look nervous,' Tushar remarked, noticing that she was silent and lost in thought. That brought her back to reality.

'No … I mean yes, you are finally meeting my brother and sister. I am not at all nervous as I know they'll love you.'

'I don't mind your sister loving me,' Tushar said teasingly.

'Shut up.' She hit him on his arm as he drove towards C Block.

'Actually, I've already met your brother. The day when Ruhi blacked out. Remember?'

'Of course. But that wasn't really a meeting. Once things got back to normal the next day, he did mention that he should have at least thanked you properly for letting him go that night.'

'I understand. By the way, your complaint has been registered. I checked.'

'Yeah, as if your department is going to get hold of the thief. They can't crack high-profile cases and I should expect them to get hold of a local burglar when no one even saw him?'

'My duty is to assure you that we will. I get paid for it.' Tushar laughed.

'You know, I was really scared till I reached home. I just can't express how I felt. I don't know what I would have done if something had happened to her. She's more like a child to me than a sister. And Kartik, he would've had a breakdown for sure. He's so attached to her.'

Tushar lifted his hand from the gear shift to hold hers consolingly for a few seconds. She had been through a lot, and seeing Kartik or Ruhi in any kind of trouble always upset her.

'You think she'll be able to make up with your dad? I mean, he has made a lot of attempts to build a normal relationship with her.'

'I don't know how to define normal. To others, we may sound crazy and arrogant, but for us, that's normal.'

She no longer regretted the separation from her father, now that she had built an independent family with her siblings—small, but a source of joy and comfort. That was what mattered after all; people could spend lifetimes searching for happiness outside their home. Moreover, now that Tushar was going to be a part of it, Dipika felt her life was complete. She was super-excited that everyone was finally meeting under one roof today.

After parking the car outside, they opened the gate to see Kartik already standing at the door to welcome them. After greeting them, he invited Tushar inside.

'Should I formally introduce you or will you do it yourselves? I'll just go and make coffee for all of us. Ruhi will be here any moment with her boyfriend,' Dipika declared.

'We're good,' Tushar assured her.

Kartik observed him for a few seconds. Tushar, feeling a little uncomfortable, decided to start the conversation himself.

'We have met before. Not the finest of places to have the first interaction, but yeah …'

Kartik smiled. 'That's what I was about to say. Sorry, my mind was on Ruhi's crisis at that time so we barely got to interact. By the way, thanks. If it wasn't for you, I would've had to have a cup of tea with the cops.'

'Oh, that's okay. Thankfully, nothing serious happened that night.'

Yeah, I'm glad … by the way, you look different without your uniform.'

'So, do I look better or worse?'

'How does it matter when you are already taken? Dipika would know … if she loves you, I'm sure you're special either way, with or without the uniform. She's quite selective in her choices.'

'Indeed, she is. I realised this the very first time I went shopping with her. That turned out to be the last time. It's been two years now.'

'What the fuck! You guys have been dating for two years and I'm getting to know about it only now?' Kartik was shocked.

'I wanted to be sure, so I took my own time,' Dipika shouted from the kitchen.

'It took you two fucking years to be sure?'

'You said it yourself. I am selective,' Dipika shot back.

'That's crazy!' Kartik ran a hand through his hair and said to Tushar, 'You should have put her behind bars.'

'Have you forgotten the main rule of relationships, my friend? The woman is always right.' Tushar smiled.

The leg-pulling continued for some time, and Dipika was happy to see Kartik gelling with Tushar. She also joined in. What more could she ask for? It looked like they were all going to be one big happy family, as she had always wished. Often, when two people meet, they take time to strike up a conversation and get along, but Kartik made friends quickly. From cricket to web series, he and Tushar continued talking casually about everything under the sun, until they were interrupted by the sound of the doorbell. Ruhi had arrived with Mihir. Everyone, including Tushar, knew that Kartik was in for a shock, as Ruhi had already discussed her relationship with Mihir in detail with Dipika, who had in turn told Tushar about it.

The moment Kartik saw Mihir at the door, his eyes widened. At first he thought it was a coincidence, but he soon recollected that Ruhi was to come home with her boyfriend.

*Holy crap. Is Mihir her boyfriend? First Dipika, who kept her affair secret for so long, and now this! It's another level of surprise. Why did I fail to sense it? Damn—so whenever he came home after work, he used to reach before me for this reason, and I used to think about how fucking punctual he is.*

'Should I?' Mihir seemed to be asking for his permission to come inside.

'Of course, it's your house. I feel like I should ask for your permission,' Kartik said sarcastically.

Ruhi couldn't contain her smile. Kartik looked at Dipika, who said, 'I knew. She told me.' Dipika too had a smile on her face.

'Now tell me, did you also know this?' Kartik turned to Tushar.

'Unfortunately, yes.' He too couldn't help but smile.

'Shit, man, you people should work for secret agencies.' Kartik still couldn't believe what was happening. He turned to Ruhi and added, 'Even you wanted to be sure?'

'No, bhai, nothing like that. I liked him since the first time we met during our college days ... when you introduced me to him. When he expressed his feelings, I told him that we should inform you. He even tried to do so. But he was afraid of your reaction ... it was only out of respect, as you are after all my brother ... *and* his best friend.'

'Kartik, my intentions are good. I genuinely had no clue how to tell you that I am dating your sister. You are my best friend and that made things more difficult.'

'Bullshit, you should have told me first. This just shows how much you trust me. You thought I would object to this? Really? You guys are silly. For me, nothing in this world is more important than Ruhi's smile. Her happiness means everything to me. If it were someone else, I wouldn't have accepted it so easily. But with you, I can blindly trust that you'll make her happy. I am just upset right now because I used to believe that we keep no secrets from each other.'

'Okay, I am sorry. You want me to go down on my knees to ask your permission?' Mihir smiled and tried to hug him.

Kartik pushed him away and said, 'Yes, please do that. Right now. Only then will I give a green signal.'

Although Kartik was teasing him, Mihir actually went down on his knees. 'Can I marry your sister in the near future?' Everyone in the room burst out laughing. For Mihir and Kartik, it was fresh proof that their friendship wasn't brittle; it stood firm on the foundation of true understanding. It was rare to find such a friendship. They hated seeing each other in a bind, they felt each other's pain without words, and always found the right words to comfort the other during difficult times.

'By the way, your love is true. The burglar that day wasn't able to steal the ring you gave Ruhi,' Tushar said with a grin.

'You see, we are made for each other ... like a match made in heaven,' said Mihir.

They were well on their way to becoming one happy family, with no complications, ego hassles or worrying thoughts of the world outside, but they were unaware of the tragic fate that was approaching. They were making plans to settle down soon, oblivious of the terrible event that would unsettle and uproot them completely. Not one of them would have believed it, if they were told that in a couple of years, their smiles would disappear and happiness would part ways with them. If only they could've predicted what the future held for them.

~

'Good morning, Kartik. How are you feeling today?' Dr Singh greeted him as they began yet another Friday session. Today, however, he didn't smile.

When Kartik merely shrugged, Dr Singh continued. 'I've told you, my job is to ask and make sure that you are feeling better. By doing so, I ensure that you're comfortable with the session.'

'Today, may I ask *you* a question?' Kartik leaned forward and placed his hands on the table. 'You didn't smile when you came in. Why is that?'

'I guess … because, in all probability, this is your last session.'

'If that's so, I can see that you aren't happy about it.'

'It's going to be a tough day for you and hence I am … perhaps a bit sceptical.' Dr Singh got up from his chair and walked over to the window. Kartik watched him, waiting for him to throw some light on what he had just said. But Dr Singh stayed silent, looking out of the window.

After some time, he turned and said, 'Kartik, when I say this will be your last session, I mean it. And when I add that it's going to be the toughest, I mean that too. When we last met, you spoke about your bond with your sisters and how the three of you managed to build a new life together. I am sure that, after the session, you must have relived all those memories ...'

'You can come to the point directly, Dr Singh,' Kartik interrupted.

'Okay, so what I want to say is ... trust me. Last time, before you opened up, you weren't sure how that would help. And even today you may not be sure, but you have to trust me. Today, I want you to go back and recall the day of 29 November. Yes, it's going to be tough ... but I want you to open up before we release you. Keep nothing in your mind. Not even the slightest thing you remember.'

Kartik broke out in goosebumps just thinking about it. Last time, he had felt better after opening up. But those had been happy memories, and he wasn't sure how he would feel now. He was determined to do it, though, perhaps because Dr Singh had said it would be his last session. *They really know how to play with your mind, these doctors*, Kartik thought. Whether or not it would really be his last session, his words had their intended impact on Kartik's mind.

Kartik thought back to the morning of 29 November. He recalled Dipika calling him at work to say that she had a very urgent meeting lined up later, and that she wouldn't be able to come home that night.

'This is not done. You know Mihir and I have arranged a surprise birthday party for Ruhi. How can the party happen without you? Why don't you just postpone the meeting?' The disappointment was evident in his voice.

'You don't need to say that to me. I tried to get out of the meeting in every way possible, but I couldn't. I'll try my best to wind things up and return by early morning so I can join you for brunch. It's a bit of an emergency at work and I have to be here,' Dipika explained.

'Don't tell me you're not sure about brunch tomorrow either? That has never happened.'

'I'll try my best,' she said with a sigh.

Kartik hung up in anger. He wanted Dipika to be there. After all, it was Ruhi's twenty-fifth birthday, and it had to be made special. Dipika's last-minute change of plan naturally upset him. The thought of cancelling the party flashed through his mind, but he didn't want to spoil the evening for Ruhi. He messaged Mihir to confirm that everything was on track. Mihir replied instantly.

*'All set. See you around nine. I have called a couple of common friends, but not sure who will be able to make it. Pooja has confirmed. Don't worry; we'll have a great evening.'*

That message put Kartik's mind at rest. He left work early to get Ruhi's birthday present gift-wrapped. It had been delivered to his office early that morning: a OnePlus 6. She had wanted one for so long. He had also bought all kinds of stuff for the party, including the booze and decorations. He pasted a special note he had written on the gift-wrapped box, and put it on the passenger seat. While he waited at a red light, music played on the car stereo and he glanced towards the note again. Rereading the words brought a smile to his face. Just to make sure Ruhi was home, he gave her a call. Ruhi picked up and said she was buying groceries at the supermarket. Then she told him that Dipika had called to say that her meeting had been postponed and she was coming home that night after all. Delighted by the news, Kartik thought of calling Dipika, but as he drove into their lane just then, he saw Ruhi across the road from their apartment, talking to someone he didn't know. It was dark, but he could make out the man's long ponytail and the white shirt he was wearing.

The fact that she was deep in conversation with someone who was a complete stranger to him surprised Kartik less than the fact that she had lied about it on the phone. It was clearly a heated argument of some sort. Kartik was just about to get out of his car when the guy walked away.

Once home, however, Kartik pretended that it was just another normal evening. He didn't say a word to Ruhi about the guy on the street or, naturally, about the party planned for that night. He didn't want to dampen her mood or spoil the surprise. And if something serious was going on with the ponytailed stranger, it could be discussed later. Kartik decided to bring it up at brunch the next day.

After making a few work calls, when Ruhi was in the kitchen, Kartik took his bag and hurried into his room to change and hide her gift in his drawer. He was really trying not to give away the surprise. It would be worth all the effort just to see her jump in joy when everyone arrived.

After putting the gift away, he happened to look out of the window as he was changing his shirt. He was astonished to see a guy outside their house, peeping in through the kitchen window. Suddenly, Kartik remembered that he had seen the same guy hanging around the apartment a few times before. His behaviour had always seemed vaguely suspicious, but Kartik had ignored him. However, now it dawned on him that he was the same man Ruhi had been talking to outside the apartment earlier in the evening; same white shirt and ponytail. Who *was* this guy? And why was Ruhi speaking with him? What had they been arguing about? And moreover, why did she have to hide the fact that she was meeting this person, preferring not to mention it even after she got home? After trying to peek in for a good five minutes, the man finally walked away. Kartik was strongly tempted to follow and confront him then and there, but he reminded himself that Ruhi was on talking terms with the guy. He had to talk to Ruhi about it first, and he would do so the next day, for sure.

~

Kartik's hands were shaking; he had folded his legs tightly under the table as the thought of the outcome of his decisions that night pulled him back to the reality of the present. He sat in Dr Singh's office feeling numb and spent.

'Would you like some water?' Dr Singh offered him a glass. Kartik took it without making eye contact with the doctor and took a sip while he struggled to calm his mind.

'You regret not talking with Ruhi that day?' Dr Singh asked.

Kartik simply nodded and was silent for a few seconds. Then he looked Dr Singh in the eye and asked, 'Do you believe me? My story?'

'Yes, I do. I believe you are not lying. I would dismiss your story if I thought otherwise. I am a psychiatrist; it's not easy to lie to me.'

'But the cops don't believe me,' Kartik said in a dejected voice.

'There are many things in life which are beyond explanation. Maybe your story is one of those,' Dr Singh tried to pacify him.

'I lost my sister. And they still don't believe me.'

'Would you mind telling me what happened at the party?' Dr Singh asked, leaning forward in his chair as if to listen more intently.

'After I had changed, I went to the parking to collect the stuff that was in the car. Mihir too had reached by then, with Pooja. Pooja was Ruhi's best friend, and the three of them often hung out together. You should have seen the joy on Ruhi's face when we burst in on her together. She really believed nothing had been planned for the night. So when she found out that we had organised a party, she was exhilarated,' Kartik said as he blinked away tears.

'Are you okay?' Dr Singh didn't want him to get too upset.

'Yeah. Just that ... you know ... I still remember how she danced like a kid on seeing her gift. She had longed for it ... Once we all were settled, we started drinking. Pizzas were ordered and I had made a playlist of all her favourite songs for the night. Time just flew as we enjoyed ourselves. One ... two ... three ... and then I lost count of the drinks I had had. I almost finished an entire bottle of whiskey. Pooja left early, around ten; she was not allowed to stay overnight.'

'So you don't remember anything that happened afterwards, right?' Dr Singh said, coaxing him to test his memory.

'All I remember was that, after she cut the cake, I had a few more drinks ... and that's it. Someone came out of her room and took me to my bedroom. But I didn't feel, even once, that there was anything unusual about her behaviour that evening ... that she was unhappy or sad about something. Rather, she seemed very content with

Mihir around; he added value to her life. Yeah, they used to fight sometimes, maybe more often than that, but which couple doesn't? That couldn't be a reason for her to kill herself. When she had so much to cherish and look forward to, why would she decide to end her life all of a sudden? The cops just made up a story because they couldn't find any evidence of foul play.'

The words, 'I'll be as free as a bird from now on; no worries, no tensions, nothing', suddenly echoed in his mind. He felt helpless; the more he thought about that night, the more guilt-ridden he was.

'I don't know if I should ask you this, but there was no mention of it in your version of what happened that night, so I thought I should.' Dr Singh got up from his seat casually and sat on the edge of the table.

Kartik looked up at him with a questioning look on his face.

'Did you know that Ruhi was pregnant?'

Kartik could not believe what Dr Singh had just said. He could feel pain moving through his body, expanding and engulfing everything inside him. Can you imagine the feeling of something so utterly repulsive moving over your skin that you have to scrape it off immediately? Now imagine it being under your skin; all you want to do is get it off but you can't, no matter how hard you try, you can't scrape it off.

'Have you lost it, Dr Singh? You are talking nonsense. She wasn't pregnant. That's impossible. You're trying to manipulate facts to make me talk. Did the cops bribe you to do this?' Kartik yelled, getting up from his seat. He was totally out of control. If it had been someone other than Dr Singh, he would have hit him.

'Calm down, Kartik. Relax.' Dr Singh made him sit back down on the chair. He took a deep breath, realising that he shouldn't have disclosed this information to Kartik. 'Why would I do that? I'm sorry. I thought you were aware of it. I am just saying what's been mentioned in the reports. I don't know how this fact has stayed hidden from you for so long.'

*Was it really true? How could it be? Does this mean that two people died that night, Ruhi and her child? No, this can't be fucking true. No one told me about it! THIS CAN'T BE FUCKING TRUE.*

'It's a lie.'

He didn't have the courage to say another word. He felt shattered and completely drained of energy, like there was this black hole inside him, consuming everything. The doctor's words had almost crushed his ribs; he had this overwhelming sensation that he was dying, slowly and painfully.

## chapter six

If depression had knocked on Kartik's door on the day Ruhi died, Dipika's life was no less painful. She felt like she was in an endless spinning wheel; afraid to take the fall and face up to what was real. She knew it was just a phase, but she prayed for it to end as she was tired of this maze that trapped her in fear. Alone in their apartment, only she knew what she had to endure, haunted by memories of Ruhi by day and the wildest nightmares by night. Her dad had even tried to take her back home, but Dipika wasn't ready for yet another debacle, knowing how her stepmother was. Eventually she shifted to another apartment. Tushar was her sole strength through all those sleepless nights.

No matter how composed she appeared to the world, she was bleeding inside. Not only had she lost a sister forever, but her brother had completely collapsed. The strain of caring for him and the regular visits to the hospital had taken their toll. However, seeing Kartik's gradual improvement also gave her hope, a reason to live. It was a lot for a young soul to bear, but Dipika had won the battle in her mind. Now that Kartik was getting discharged in a week, she was happy, but also worried. After several months in the hospital, recovering from his breakdown, he would be seeing the light of the outside world for the very first time after Ruhi's death. She wanted to make sure that there were no setbacks. To help smoothen the transition, she and Tushar had met Mihir to ask for his moral support.

'You don't have to tell me that. I've always stood by him in the past, and I will continue to do that. He's my best friend,' Mihir said firmly, as he offered glasses of water to Dipika and Tushar.

'I know, but things aren't the same ... so we thought we'd have a word with you,' Tushar explained. 'How's Pooja?'

'She is fine. We have all had a tough time.' Placing the tray on the table, Mihir sat down next to them.

'The doctors have said that they'll call me and dad sometime next week to sign the release papers. What I'm worried about is that ... during his last session, he got to know that Ruhi was pregnant.'

'What?' That shocked Mihir; his eyes widened.

'I don't know how to face him now. I had taken the utmost care to keep it a secret from him by telling everyone, including the cops, not to let him know, giving his health as the reason. Even the last time he was interrogated, I had managed to keep the cops silent about it but ...' Dipika shook her head. She knew her brother would be furious that everyone except him knew about it. She couldn't justify keeping the truth from him by citing his health, not to Kartik.

'Fuck, I didn't know this. You were right not to tell him; it wasn't the right time for him to find out. I hope it doesn't upset him too much.' Mihir's expression showed how anxious he was. He realised that he hadn't really wanted Kartik to know. After all, it didn't matter anymore.

'Let me know when they are releasing him,' Mihir continued. 'I'll be there. But why did they interrogate him again? Did the doctors allow it?'

'The police are interrogating everyone involved in the case once again. And the doctors thought it was all right because of his improvement. Perhaps they hoped this would be an opportunity for him to let it all out,' Tushar said. 'By the way, I have heard from a few inside sources that you'll be next. It's just a formality to close the case permanently. I don't know the details, as I have been kept away from the case.'

The department hadn't involved Tushar in the case despite his being on the Gurgaon team, because his relationship with the family could give rise to a conflict of interest. They wanted to keep the investigation free of bias or prejudice.

'Okay,' Mihir said, nodding. He turned to Dipika and asked, 'What reason will you give him for not telling him about Ruhi's pregnancy?' He sounded worried. 'He'll feel terrible that he has got to know about it after more than half a year.'

'I'm sure you'll be able to convince him that it was for the best,' Tushar reassured Dipika. 'You are good at that.'

'Too many things to convince him about; first the stalker, and now this. I don't know how I'll do it ...' Dipika confessed.

'He still believes there was someone stalking her?'

'Unfortunately, yes.'

~

Time is our birth right and our only luxury; it's also a curse when we can't bring back the past or the loved ones we have lost. Destiny cannot be erased, any more than a birthmark at the centre of the forehead. Looking back, Mihir remembered the smiles that he had once shared with Ruhi, how her face had brightened with love when their eyes met. Vivid thoughts of her overwhelmed him, and he felt that, sometimes, seconds could be like lifetimes, and yet minutes briskly swept by. It felt like several lifetimes ago but he remembered everything about her; mostly, how innocently she used to place her head on his chest, tracing circles over his heart like rings around Saturn, and how she made him feel like he was her whole universe.

After Dipika and Tushar had left, Mihir sat reminiscing about how they had met for the first time in a public library. He had downed four cups of coffee, trying hard to concentrate on his studies, but the caffeine didn't seem to be working that day. The library in Gurgaon was one of the places where he felt like he truly belonged. That, and his bed. His definition of an ideal vacation was being able to read books in peace. To him, fiction always felt real, and nonfiction seemed far from realistic. He wasn't a nerd as such, but he was one of those guys who opened up only to his closest friends. For others, he seemed to carry the label, 'lost in himself, don't bother'.

But for now, he had to keep fiction aside and concentrate on his textbooks. *One … two … three … concentrate, concentrate!* He repeated this in his mind, trying hard to focus on his studies. However, all his attempts failed the moment he saw a girl entering the library and taking a seat a few tables away from him. Her looks drew his attention instantly; Mihir couldn't help but observe that she didn't have an hourglass figure, but her aura of simplicity and innocence made his heart beat faster. She wasn't one of those Instagram models who mask themselves with plastic beauty, but she had that girl-next-door look and expressions that made him long to know more about her. She would look ordinary or imperfect in front of those so-called beauties, but her imperfection had its own charm. With her strikingly simple attire and sharp features, she certainly couldn't go unnoticed.

Every time she looked up, he found it hard not to blush. In all these years, he had never felt such an adrenaline rush in the presence of a girl. She had a glow that his vocabulary simply couldn't describe, he felt. The longer he looked at her, the more he fell in love with her. It was instant. He wondered who she was; he was a regular at the library but he hadn't seen her there before. Now his concentration was back but it was not on his books. He simply flipped through the pages, pretending to read but actually gazing at her. A couple of times when she looked at him, he quickly turned his head, not wanting to make his attraction so obvious. All he wanted was to go up to the girl and speak to her. But if he'd had the guts to do that, he wouldn't be single till date, Mihir reminded himself.

*Should I or shouldn't I? If I just go and strike up a conversation, will I look like a desperate single guy who runs after every hot girl? But such despos aren't found in libraries. She would be sensible enough to understand that, I think. But will it be of any use? She is drop-dead gorgeous, she might not even be single. And even if she is, how does it matter? I'm sure she wouldn't pay me any heed. Fuck dude, how am I even a Delhi guy, I can't even approach a girl. No fucking Delhi qualities in me.*

She left after some time and Mihir cursed himself. All he had done was debate in his own mind. *Am I even a guy*, he thought. Then he reminded himself that, in most cases, boys don't succeed with girls because of their hesitant attitude. *One should keep trying; let luck do the rest.* He didn't have to wait long, as the very next day he spotted her again in the library; this time she was already there when he walked in.

*Has she noticed me too? I came here just for her; did she come for the same reason? Or is it all in my mind?*

He was so engrossed in her that he didn't notice at first that she was with someone. For a minute, his hopes were dashed. Then the guy turned and he saw his face. Mihir was stunned; she was with Kartik, his best friend.

*What the fuck? Is she his girlfriend? He never told me that he was in a relationship. Why does this happen to me? I had barely begun to picture her in my mind, and now it all has to end on the second day?*

He just stood there, staring at both of them, when Kartik saw him and waved. He was equally surprised to see Mihir there. They had been best friends for the last couple of years, but Kartik hadn't known he was a regular at this library. As far as Mihir knew, Kartik didn't like coming to libraries; that's what he claimed whenever his friend suggested going to the college library.

'What are you doing here?' Mihir finally found his voice.

'I told you that we've shifted here to C Block in Gurgaon. Ruhi took a membership here yesterday, so I just came to have a look. And trust me, it's as boring as our college library,' Kartik said with a laugh.

'She is ...?' Mihir asked hesitantly, his fingers crossed in the hope that she wasn't Kartik's girlfriend.

'Oh, I forgot to make introductions. This is my sister, Ruhi.'

'Oh, thank God she is your sister.' Mihir's involuntary sigh was loud enough for Ruhi as well as Kartik to notice.

'Sorry?' Kartik gave him a look.

'I said … so, she is your sister. I mean … this is the first time I am meeting someone from your family since we became friends.'

'I have invited you so many times to my house, but you will be you. Lazy ass.'

Mihir knew Ruhi had instantly understood what his intentions were. She said nothing, but had a faint smile on her face, which made him smile too. No one can beat girls when it comes to insights into human psychology, Mihir thought.

'By the way, why don't you come to our house the day after tomorrow? It's Sunday and Ruhi's friend Pooja is coming over too. We could hang out, have fun,' Kartik suggested.

Mihir couldn't have asked for anything better. He could have kissed Kartik if Ruhi hadn't been standing right there. But what came next almost paralysed his tongue and stopped his heart.

'Yeah, you should,' Ruhi said in her soft, melodious voice.

He had always dreamed that, someday, someone would come along and set a fire burning in his heart, someone who was going to give him a reason to say 'I love you'. Someday, someone was going to give him a new beginning. With all his heart, he hoped Sunday would be that day.

~

It's strange how an emotion as strong as love can also be your greatest weakness. It just needs a moment, and in that moment, sometimes you see a lifetime's worth of love. Mihir wanted to be with someone whose heart beat faster with his gentle caresses, whose breath stopped with just one glance at him, whose palms sweat because her nerves got the better of her in his presence. He wanted to be with someone who struggled to suppress a shy smile every time he smiled at her, a smile that was reserved only for her. After meeting Ruhi for the first time, he felt that perhaps he had found that someone and wanted to give it a try. He had never felt like this before, and he didn't want to risk leaving things to fate.

It was Sunday evening and he was already on his way to Kartik's, looking very dapper in a black casual shirt. He hated wearing shirts, but he wore one that day as he had a hunch that a special someone would love it. He didn't have to wait long at the door. The moment he rang the bell, Ruhi opened the door.

'She was waiting for you,' a girl he assumed was Pooja shouted from behind her.

'For me? I'm sure you're kidding,' Mihir responded immediately.

'No, trust me. Since I got here, all I've been hearing about is you,' Pooja said with a grin. 'Kartik's friend is coming; we have to do this and that; blah, blah … she has made Dipika slave away in the kitchen since the afternoon, I heard—'

'Don't take her seriously,' Ruhi interrupted.

Mihir could hardly believe what Pooja was saying, anyway; he hadn't dared to hope that Ruhi could actually feel the same way about him. And if a tiny shred of hope remained, it disappeared when Dipika also said in response to Pooja's leg-pulling antics, 'She's crazy, ignore her.' All Mihir could do was smile.

It was true; no one took Pooja seriously anyway. People who didn't know her tended to think she was stupid, but her friends and family loved her for being so lively all the time. Often, she was dismissed as loud and melodramatic, but Pooja didn't care what anyone said about her. It worked the other way too; she had her own opinions about people, but she rarely criticised others. In fact, she always tried to say positive things about them. That was just how she was; often, she wasn't even conscious about this behaviour. And her friends loved her for it.

As Mihir took his seat, Pooja continued, 'So, you do like her?' That took him completely by surprise.

*Yes, I do. I do like her a lot. What the fuck am I supposed to say? I can't just go along with this leg-pulling. Control yourself, Mihir.* His mind raced.

'Yeah, I mean … she is my friend's sister, so …'

Pooja cut him short. 'Come on, dude. I know you do like her.'

In fact, Ruhi had caught him staring at her that day at the library. She had discussed it at length with Pooja, who wanted to tease Mihir about it. She was now enjoying the sight of Mihir getting roasted.

Kartik had been in the shower since his friend's arrival. His appearance interrupted their fun and Mihir was temporarily rescued from the teasing.

'Thank you so much for rescuing me. These girls are crazy. Women empowerment is taking a different route altogether these days, I must say. Female dominance is dangerous for guys like me,' Mihir said light-heartedly.

Kartik laughed, and Dipika too joined in, and soon the formal introductions were done. It didn't take long for them to open up to each other. As the evening wore on, it seemed as if old friends were having a reunion. Dipika and Kartik made everyone comfortable, and Pooja could even make friends with a pizza delivery boy in a matter of minutes. As the hours passed, they not only got to know each other better, but realised that they loved being in each other's company. It takes warmth and effort to make a home out of a house, and the youngsters gathered at the Gurgaon C Block apartment that night were nailing it. It's rightly said that there is nothing on this earth more to be prized than true friendship.

After dinner, Mihir was standing on the balcony after making a call, when he saw Ruhi coming up to him with two cups of coffee. He was on cloud nine. He hadn't expected to have an after-dinner conversation over coffee with Ruhi, that too within such a short duration of having met her.

'Talking to your girlfriend?' she asked, offering him a cup.

'No, it was my mother. She keeps calling every few hours to check on me. It's irritating sometimes.' Mihir took the cup from her.

'I wish my mother was alive. I wouldn't have waited for her to call; I would have done it myself. Ask me … I'll tell you how much I miss that irritating motherly care.'

Mihir realised that he shouldn't have said what he had. 'I'm sorry for your loss. Isn't it strange how we don't realise the value of a loved one until we lose them?'

Ruhi didn't say anything. To lighten the mood, Mihir changed the topic. 'So, do you have a boyfriend?'

'No, I need time.'

*Did she think that I am asking her out? She needs time for what?*

He said, 'Sorry, I didn't get you …?'

'I mean, I need time for all this … love affairs and relationships. It's not something to show off … having a boyfriend. When I'm mentally prepared for it, I'll think about it. All my life, I have always seen relationships break … be it my parents' or my friends'. It takes a lot out of you. So, I need time.' Ruhi was being absolutely straightforward with him.

Mihir sighed, realising that it was indeed too soon for him as well. It also struck him that one wrong decision in this matter could spoil his friendship with Kartik, and he didn't want that to happen. Finally, he respected the fact that Ruhi needed time; she was absolutely right in saying so. He would have to be patient; that's how relationships worked. All Mihir could do was wait and hope that Ruhi would write a happy ending to his love story.

## chapter seven

When you lose someone you love, it's like losing a part of yourself forever. That portion of you simply can't be restored, and there are some days when you just can't stop thinking about them. The more you try not to, the more you are pulled into the memories you had shared. The day when Dipika and Tushar visited his house was one of those days for Mihir; everything reminded him of Ruhi. To divert his mind, he called Pooja, but all they did was talk about her.

'Dipika called; she said that Kartik is getting discharged next week and also that you would be called in for another interrogation sometime this week,' Pooja said. 'I don't know what to say. You think if I could have stayed over that night, things would have been different?'

'We can't stop things from happening if they are destined to happen. At least you were not dragged into the police investigation because you left early and the security guard saw you leaving. Or else, like me, you would also have had to go through these shitty interrogations. As if anything's going to change because of them ...'

'Just stay calm. Try not to get troubled by all these things. We all have had to go through enough.'

'I know.' Mihir sighed.

'I still remember the day you proposed to her. Things were so different then. Look at us now. I feel so guilty about not staying back that night. Do you blame me for what happened?'

'It's not your fault. We're all blaming ourselves. Dipika has her reasons, Kartik has his. The same goes for you. Whatever happened had to happen. That's the reality of life. There's nothing you or I could have done. We did the right thing. Everyone must move on, keeping only the happy memories. I hope Kartik is able to cope, once he's out.' Mihir tried his best to persuade Pooja not to feel responsible for what had happened. She wasn't allowed to stay away from home overnight, and her decision to leave early was quite understandable. On some level, he was also impelling himself to push away his own feelings of guilt about that day. It's often said that if you wish for something from the bottom of your heart, the universe conspires to make it possible. Sadly, it's the same for consuming thoughts that you want to get rid of. The more you try to wish them away, the more the universe contrives to throw them back at you.

That evening, while looking for something in his drawer, he happened to see the gold ring that he had gifted Ruhi on her birthday a couple of years ago.

She had asked for a diamond ring on her twenty-fifth birthday. As he stared at the ring, his vision blurred. His mind took a trip down memory lane to the day he had proposed to her. She needed time, she had said, and he had waited for one long year for that moment to arrive. In that one year, their relationships had all grown stronger. Mihir had been best friends with Pooja since the day they'd met. Doesn't it happen sometimes? Somehow, you instantly become comfortable with the friends of the one you love. As for Ruhi, Mihir had not only gotten closer to her but had also gained her trust. He had almost become a part of her family by now. It was the right time to take the relationship a step further, he thought.

'We are meeting in the library. I asked her to come alone. But I am nervous as hell. You have to come along. I can't even tell Kartik.' Mihir was on the phone with Pooja. He was about to reveal his feelings to Ruhi for the first time and needed moral support.

'You'll propose, she'll accept, and what am I supposed to do there? Clap for your new beginning?' Pooja teased.

'This is not done … we three have been friends for a year now. You can't leave me alone to die of nervousness,' Mihir insisted. He was already on his way.

'You have to do it alone, my boy. You certainly won't invite me to go along on your first date. Will you?'

'I will. I promise.'

'Shut up and just go. By the way, she's already got the hint from the sudden change in your behaviour. She called me some time ago.'

'Fuck, are you serious?' Mihir almost had a panic attack.

'Yeah, she said, "Mihir has asked me to meet him at the library; maybe he is going to propose".' Pooja said. She couldn't control her laugher.

'And what did you say? What did she say? Is her answer yes?' Mihir was definitely panicking now.

'Go and hear it directly from the horse's mouth.'

'Please tell me.'

'I won't.'

'Do you mean that she is going to refuse?'

After a brief pause, Pooja replied in a muffled voice, 'I don't know. She isn't sure yet. That's what I felt.'

'Why the fuck did I even call you? You should support me, not pull me down like this.' He was almost shouting on the phone now.

'Why the hell did you ask me then? Don't worry, you'll convince her. I know you well by now ... better than her,' Pooja tried to console Mihir. By this time he had reached the library and he hung up.

Ruhi was there already. Just one look from her made him go into a sort of trance. There was something undefinable about her which made him go crazy. He couldn't, for the life of him, put that feeling into words, but he was madly in love.

The conversation with Pooja had taken a toll on his confidence, but he knew that if it didn't happen today, it would never come to pass. And yet, if she said no, he would lose his best friend. He decided to forget the outcome and lay his heart open in front of her with the hope that she wouldn't crush it. In some way, he even loved the anxiety that he was experiencing now, as such moments never return once a relationship commences. It was somewhat like examination results. Once you see your name on the list, within a fraction of a second you know whether you have passed or failed. Either way, there would be an end to the anxiety of not knowing.

'Please sit.' By saying this to Ruhi, Mihir was actually trying to compose himself.

Ruhi just gazed at him, as if she wanted to know what exactly he wanted to say.

'Remember, you had told me when we first met that you needed time to fall in love. You said that you weren't mentally prepared for a relationship.' Mihir was trying to build a foundation for the main part.

'Yes, I remember. But what exactly do you want to say?' Ruhi sounded confused.

'What I mean is ... don't you think that such things are beyond our control? You meet someone, spend some time with them and you start falling for that person. You love being with that person; you love everything about them. Don't you think so?'

How desperately he wanted to hear 'yes'! He wanted her to understand that he loved her. Yet, if there was one thing he had learnt after falling in love, it was the value of patience.

'Yeah ... it happens. But you know, falling in love at first sight is something I don't believe in,' Ruhi explained.

'So ... now that we've known each other for one year, do you think it's the right time?'

*Fuck, I shouldn't have said that. No, just say it, speak up! It was like Mihir had two conflicting voices in his head.*

'Sorry, right time for what?' Ruhi was playing with him; she knew where the conversation was heading, but she wanted to hear it from him.

'I don't know how to say it, you are my friend's sister ... but you know what I mean, right?'

*Speak up. Be a man!*

'You know I love reading romantic novels, right? The way the characters express themselves, the way they love ... you too have read many books. But here you are, doing nothing special ... and you want me to say that I know. That's not happening.'

*It's a yes, it's a yes. I want to shout to the world that I have fucking done it. Pooja was wrong. It's a fucking yes.*

'I know your taste,' Mihir said with a smile, and added, 'I have a surprise. But for that, you need to go to the romance section of the library and pick out your favourite book.'

Ruhi couldn't comprehend what exactly he had in mind, but went to the rack and picked up the book she loved the most. Mihir knew about her favourite book as she had mentioned it more than a couple of times over the past year. She came back with the book and sat facing him. Mihir signalled to her to open the book. It had a special note pasted inside it. A few hours earlier, he had come to the library to slip into her favourite romantic novel, *P.S. I Love You*, a note that expressed all his feelings. He knew she was an avid reader and what better way to propose to her than to put it in writing, that too inside her favourite book. Ruhi was flabbergasted, but she had a smile on her face that he had never seen before.

*'At first, I thought it's not right. So, like you, I took my time. But the more time I spend with you, the stronger my feelings grow. I am overwhelmed by your perfection. Like the finest creation of God's hands. I don't think there has been a single day since we met that you have not been in my thoughts. When I look into your eyes, I feel like nothing but love can exist between us. You fill me with love, trust and desire. Even if you return my feelings and the fire of what you feel for me dies someday, I cannot imagine that the passion I have for you will ever dim. It is like the rarest of gems. I cannot begin to recollect if I have ever felt this happy or vulnerable. And your happiness is of utmost importance to me; when I see your smile, I can overlook all the darkness and decay of the real world. Every heartbeat of mine speaks your name, screams 'I love you'. I really do. I don't want a happy ending; I want a never-ending relationship. Will you love me the way I love you?'*

Ruhi blushed, looking down at the note, and nodded. Mihir was speechless; it was finally happening. The sudden silence that engulfed them had pure love in it. Mihir took her hands in his; the touch sent shivers through both of them and she couldn't suppress her shy smile.

'I love you,' Mihir said. 'I've loved you since the moment I saw you. Whenever I look at you, I see my whole future before me. In you, I see a partner for life. No matter whether times are good or bad, I want you by my side.'

'I love you too.'

She didn't say anything else, but those were the words Mihir had craved to hear from her for so long. He felt like he had conquered the world. He had so much to say to her, but for the moment, he just kissed her hand and felt that nothing could ever go wrong in his world with her by his side.

'Did you call Pooja before coming here?' he asked, suddenly remembering what Pooja had said about Ruhi being unsure.

'No, why? Did you tell her that we were meeting?' Ruhi asked curiously.

'I did. Well, I am not going to spare her.'

He wished he'd realised that it was just a prank. It was Pooja, after all.

'Why?' Ruhi asked, confused.

'Nothing.' What could he have said, anyhow?

'Should we tell Dipika and Kartik?' Ruhi wanted them to know; after all, they were her whole world and she wanted to share her happiness with them.

'We will, but at the right time. I'll speak to Karthik when the opportunity arises. I don't know how he will react at this moment, and I don't want to spoil it for us. Trust me, I will tell him soon. And I'll convince him to accept our relationship.'

Reassured by Mihir's words, Ruhi agreed. After spending some more time together at the library, she suggested that he go home with her. Both Kartik and Dipika were out for work. Once they were in the apartment, time seemed to fly. Mihir wanted the moments to slow down almost to the point of stopping. He wanted to be alone with her forever; Ruhi felt the same. Together, they were living the most precious hours of their lives; it had been a long wait, but worth it. His hands twitched with the longing to touch her. Their gazes met, and he found himself drifting closer and closer to her, until her lips were just within reach.

'You want this?' he asked. He wanted to be sure that he didn't rush her into it. It was a special feeling and he wanted it to remain that way. Ruhi simply nodded. Her eyes spoke a million words. It was pure ecstasy that he saw in them.

He could feel her breath getting heavier as he ran his hand through her hair. She leaned in and closed her eyes. Their lips finally met, and it was a heavenly feeling like he had never known before. Mihir moved forward until her back was against the wall. It startled her.

'Shh …' Mihir whispered. 'It's all right, don't worry and just relax.'

He was slow, rhythmic and gentle, and after a brief sharp pain, a sweet spasm went through her, and she seemed to rise into the air with an incredible feeling. Ruhi was trembling. This was not familiar terrain, but she felt ready to explore it. This passion was part of their need for each other. It was love.

Even today, her bedsheets probably retained the smell of their love, he thought. Each and every moment they had shared was burned into his consciousness, concealed deep in his heart. Every beautiful memory played in his head like soft music, memories of a time that would never be forgotten but didn't last, memories that could not be undone. He put her gold ring back in his drawer. Then he resumed his day, moving on with real life. But if only for a moment, a fleeting moment, he wondered, one could feel the embrace of a loved one who is no more, what would it be like?

## chapter eight

'Mihir Ahuja, I hope you know why you have been called here?' Inspector Sunil Kumawat, who was sitting across the table from Mihir, asked in a stern voice, his eyes still on his mobile phone.

'Yes,' Mihir replied.

'So, can you tell me how you knew Ruhi?'

Once again, Mihir went over the statement that he had given them at the beginning of the police investigation into Ruhi's death.

'We met through Kartik at a public library in C Block, Gurgaon.'

'And can you tell me about the nature of your relationship with Ruhi? The reports that were filed during the investigation say that you were her boyfriend. Is that correct?' he asked. There was a grim tone to his voice.

'Ruhi ... Ruhi was my world. After our first meeting, we became good friends. She wasn't ready for a relationship then, and hence I didn't tell her about my feelings. But after a year, when I thought the time was right, I proposed to her and we got into a relationship.'

More than the questions, it was Inspector Kumawat's attitude that was pissing him off. Mihir knew such interrogations were part of their daily routine, but he wished the policemen wouldn't use that tone. However, he knew he had no choice but to swallow his irritation.

'Isn't that a long time? Waiting for a whole year ...'

'That's personal,' Mihir muttered.

'Nothing is personal; this isn't your bedroom. This is my police station and you are here for an interrogation. I expect you to put the facts in front of us,' Inspector Kumawat reacted in his stern way.

*What am I supposed to say to him? If someone waits for a long time for someone, he's doubted, and if someone doesn't wait and moves on, he is a bad character.*

'It was a long time, but I respected her space. I wanted her to be mentally prepared for a relationship. After her father's second marriage, her faith in relationships had been damaged,' Mihir explained.

'Okay. So once you got into a relationship, you've mentioned that you disclosed it to Kartik only after a year. Why was that?' It was clear that Inspector Kumawat was carefully going through every minute detail of the case, connecting the past and present statements given by everyone involved.

'We were nervous about his reaction. Even when Ruhi finally told him about us, I wasn't prepared. Luckily, he had no issues with it. We were like a family.' With each question, Mihir felt his threshold for patience decreasing.

'Your friend Kartik still believes that she didn't kill herself. He claims that it was a murder. Do you feel the same way?' Inspector Kumawat had finally begun the grilling session. His style of interrogation was different from the earlier team's methods, and he was asking uncomfortable questions in order to elicit fresh information.

'I don't know. Till I left the house that night, things seemed pretty normal. All I can say is that the person who took Kartik to his bedroom was me and not the stalker.'

He had given the same statement previously, dismissing Kartik's suspicions and explaining that it was he who had taken Kartik to his bedroom before he had passed out. After making sure that Ruhi was in her room, he had closed the door and come back to the living room to sit with Kartik for a while as he had almost drunk himself senseless. Like a true friend, Mihir had given him his shoulder to lean on. Once Kartik was in bed, he had left.

However, Inspector Kumawat had a different take on the events of that night. 'So, why did you say, "I'll be a free bird"? Kartik said that the person who took him to the bedroom came out of Ruhi's room and spoke these words. Does that mean you had already killed Ruhi by then?'

'Why the hell would I do that? He was drunk … I never uttered those words. She was my whole world. We loved each other. First your investigation team says it was suicide. Now, after so many months, you start interrogating us again and suddenly you think *I* killed her. I don't know how framing me helps this case, but seriously ... it's insane. You've just made a joke out of Ruhi's death by harassing her loved ones.'

Mihir had had enough. He stood up from his chair in frustration, then paused, took a deep breath to cool down and said, 'I don't even know the meaning of those words.'

Inspector Kumawat ordered him to sit down again, adding, 'You want to know the meaning, I will tell you. You knew Ruhi was pregnant. That meant trouble for you. If it wasn't a suicide, you were the last person to come out of her room that night. You weren't prepared to accept the child, and hence you probably killed her.'

'Inspector ... this is crazy. I told you that when I left, things were normal.' Mihir was struggling to stay calm.

'You knew Ruhi was pregnant with your child, right? Why didn't you tell Kartik or Dipika that night? Dipika came to know about it only after Ruhi's death. Kartik wasn't informed till now because the doctors said the shock of such news would destroy his mental health. You knew she was carrying your child,' Inspector Kumawat repeated, his voice raised to drive home his point.

'Yes, I knew she was pregnant. And Ruhi knew she was pregnant. But the truth is, it wasn't my child. She had confessed this to me. It was a guilt that she carried inside her every minute, for months.'

For a few moments, even Inspector Kumawat was speechless. He wasn't expecting that; it wasn't in any of the reports.

'Why didn't you mention this earlier when you were interrogated?' the inspector finally asked.

'Because I didn't want to spoil my relationship with those who are still alive or ruin the memory of the one who had gone forever. They were the only ones who could have supported me during that phase. I had already lost Ruhi, and I didn't want to lose them. Anyway, how would it have mattered? It would have only made things worse for me on a personal level.' Mihir's words were greeted with a blank stare from Inspector Kumawat.

Though his intentions were good, his timing had certainly been disastrous on both occasions, Mihir realised.

Inspector Kumawat appeared to be deep in thought. After a while, he said, 'You said everything was going well in your relationship. Didn't you?' Folding his hands, the inspector leaned back in his chair, waiting for an answer. Mihir could see that he wanted to know whether it was this guilt that had led Ruhi to take her own life. And if not, then what was it?

'Yes, it was. Everything was perfect till a couple of years ago. On her twenty-third birthday, we told Kartik and Dipika about our relationship. I had given her a gold ring with a promise to get her a diamond one on her twenty-fifth. If I had known it would be her last birthday ...'

Mihir could feel Ruhi's presence even now, if he pondered over their memories deeply. It was a feeling that weighed heavily on his heart. It was as if a part of her soul still occupied the crevasses and cracks of his. If only he had told everyone everything back then, perhaps everything would still be the way it was before. He sat there in front of Inspector Kumawat with a heavy soul, wishing he could undo what had already been done.

'I want you to run through the last couple of years of your relationship.'

Inspector Kumawat ordered two cups of tea. Mihir knew it wasn't going to be banker's hours for him today.

~

Emotions are like the tides of the sea; they have their ups and downs. And you never knew when calm waves would churn in a storm. Mihir felt that storm brewing inside him now. On the surface, he had appeared calm for the past few months, but here he was again, and a part of him wanted to scream until there wasn't a single breath left in his lungs, until it pierced the world with the energy he had expended and his words hung in the air for all to hear.

Everything had been perfect till a couple of years ago, Mihir told the inspector. Kartik had readily accepted their relationship as he had complete faith in his best friend. Dipika had no issues either. Pooja and Mihir had got along like a house on fire since the day they met. After Ruhi and Mihir started dating, whenever they fought or argued, Pooja played the mediator, helping them to work through their differences. They seemed like the perfect couple at first, complementing each other in many important ways. No matter the obstacles, they loved, laughed and did all the crazy things that kept their passion alive. Mihir wore his heart on his sleeve and was head over heels in love with Ruhi. Kartik and Dipika loved the way he pampered her. Seeing their sister happy and content made them overjoyed.

But, as time passed, their differences grew. The things that they once liked about each other became a little less charming; even 'good night' messages became irritating. They still loved each other madly, but the relationship turned platonic. Initially, they used to spend hours talking to each other; with time, that changed. Where earlier they used to exchange every single update of their daily activities, they now made do with a few quick chats. They began taking each other for granted. In the beginning, when they had fights, one of them made it a point to let things go, but later, they would stop talking to each other for hours or even days. Little differences then turned into serious quarrels, and slowly, ego started to gain the upper hand over love. They even broke up for a few days, but when they realised they still loved each other deeply, they couldn't stay apart. Their hearts didn't mend overnight, but that realisation was enough to salvage the relationship. Back together, the world again looked positive; everything around them turned beautiful and the petty problems of life seemed inconsequential. Such is the power of love.

However, a few months before Ruhi's death, Mihir sensed something fishy. She had started ignoring him a bit lately, and she seemed to panic whenever he happened to touch her phone. He began to suspect she was hiding something. But what was it? This had never happened before even during the worst of their fights. Even in normal situations, like ordering food or booking a cab, she wouldn't allow him to look at her phone. Initially, he ignored it, but when it started happening quite regularly, he was certain that there was something that she didn't want him to see. Even her photo gallery now had a pass-code, making him even more suspicious. Concerned, he began keeping a constant check on her. He didn't like doing it, but he had to know what was on her mind. Everything in his life came to a standstill a month or so before her death, when he spotted her with a guy at Ambience Mall. When they met the next day, he secretly checked her WhatsApp messages when she was in the kitchen. A message from a contact saved as 'SA' caught his attention.

*'I'll not hurt you like he does. I know he doesn't love you anymore; he is just faking it. I am so glad that you believed me. I'll not break your trust like he does. I'll not stab you unknowingly like he does. I care for you genuinely and will never ever do something that'll break your heart. I didn't want you to go on feeling cheated; that's why I came into your life. Whenever you need me, I'll be there. Please take care.'*

That message sent shivers down Mihir's spine. He couldn't believe what he had just read. Before he could note down the number, Ruhi came out of the kitchen. But the naked truth was in front of him. He felt shattered; his thoughts and emotions twisted into intricate spider webs that stretched to give him unbearable pain. He tried to confront her about it but she dismissed it, saying, 'It's not really what you are thinking. Give me a few days and I'll tell you. But it's really not like that.'

However, nothing made sense to him anymore. For the next few days, he was heartbroken. Thinking about it only made him go crazy, and so he stopped thinking. He simply let things unfold the way they had to. All he knew was that he loved her unconditionally, and he continued to do so till the day that his heart was crushed completely.

He had convinced himself that she was no longer hiding anything from him, and had gotten over what he'd seen. But the ugly truth was hiding under the sheets. He remembered that day very well; how could he forget? Ruhi hadn't been feeling well for a few days and they had gone for a check-up. He wouldn't have gone with her if he had known about the unpleasant surprise that awaited him there.

The doctors revealed that Ruhi was expecting. Mihir was in shock. It couldn't be true! How could it be? They hadn't been sleeping together for the last few months, so how could the tests be positive? It was only then that Ruhi confessed that it wasn't his child. That truth hit him like a storm; her words, like thunder and gusts of wind, pounded at the barriers of his heart until the knowledge of what had happened came flooding in through every pore of his being.

Mihir had nothing to say when he heard the news, but it weighed on his heart so much that he decided to part ways with Ruhi. He felt there was hardly any scope for sorting things out and, without a second thought, he just blocked her out of his life. Ruhi tried to talk to him and make peace, admitting that she had made a mistake. But even if it had been a mistake, Mihir had decided that it couldn't be forgiven. However, neither she nor he revealed the news of her pregnancy to Kartik or Dipika. For an entire week, Mihir avoided Kartik, who kept insisting that he join them for dinner or for an outing. Every time he invited him over, Mihir made excuses that he was working late; he simply didn't want to face Ruhi. But he loved her. Though he tried very hard to delete the memories of their love and kill his affection for her, he couldn't stop thinking about her. Thoughts of her constantly revolved around in his head.

*Why? What is it about you that leaves a lingering effect? I don't want this. I keep dreaming of you, all these different dreams. In some, you're so close to me that I can touch you; in others, you're the furthest thing I can see that's still in focus. Round and round, you spin in my head. I don't even know what exactly I'm thinking of when I'm thinking of you. I spend my time thinking about not thinking about you and I'm just caught in a loop. I hope you're okay, I hope you're safe, I hope you've eaten today, I hope you sleep well, I hope you're healthy. When will these feelings and thoughts fade? How can I spend so much time thinking about someone to whom our relationship didn't matter? I don't hate you for this, but it still hurts.*

These thoughts kept burning inside his head every single minute. He wanted to forget her, but the more he tried, the more he felt pulled to her. He even considered telling her to have an abortion, so they could get back together. But what was the unborn child's fault in all this, he thought. He couldn't kill someone who hadn't even come into this world. That child deserved life. Mihir felt caught up in a trap from which there was no escape. It is rightly said love can be your greatest strength, but it can also be your biggest weakness. Finally, Mihir gave in to his truest emotion. He stopped bothering about society, his self-respect or his foolishness. When, even after a couple of weeks he couldn't put her out of his mind, and his love for her didn't seem to fade even a bit, he decided to go back to her.

Meanwhile, Ruhi had been pleading with him to come back; she needed him more than ever before. She had sworn that she wasn't even on talking terms with the other guy. It was just a mistake and she would never ever break his trust again. To someone not in love, this would have sounded ridiculous, but Mihir was still in love. More than anything else in the world, he wanted to be by her side. If he had asked any of his friends for advice at that point, each one of them would have suggested that he move on. But when you are in love, you don't think about practical choices. It all comes down to that one damn thing that beats inside your body, keeping you alive. It has made people do the craziest things in the world; this was certainly one of them, but he didn't care anymore.

Soon, they were together again, but they still hadn't disclosed the news about Ruhi's pregnancy to Kartik and Dipika. Mihir knew it was just a matter of time before Ruhi started showing. Hence, he decided to say that the baby was his. He didn't want Kartik or Dipika to think otherwise, for they both loved Ruhi like a child and finding out that Ruhi had become pregnant out of an affair with someone else would have shattered them even more than it had Mihir. Thus, after discussing it with Ruhi, he decided to tell them on her birthday that they were making their relationship official. A couple of years ago, he had promised Ruhi that he would give her a diamond ring and formally propose. But what Ruhi was really emotional about was the fact that he had decided to tell them that it was his child. On the one hand, she felt terribly guilty about what had happened, and on the other, she felt really blessed to have someone like Mihir in her life. It seemed as if one of those characters she had so far encountered only in the love stories she liked to read had actually come to life. She was so overwhelmed by his decision that she had no words to describe her feelings. A few nights before the party, she asked him whether he was sure that this was what he wanted to do.

'As sure as I am of the fact that I love you. I want you in my life, and the child needs you to bring it to life. You are its mother. You certainly don't want to abandon a child like your dad did. So if we all need each other for a happy life, why back out? I don't know how everyone will react to your pregnancy. Maybe, initially, they will be upset, but I am sure things will be fine eventually. There's absolutely no need to tell them everything.'

On the night of the 29th, Mihir, accompanied by Pooja, reached Ruhi's house on time. Seeing Mihir, Kartik and Pooja at the door, Ruhi was delighted. She was a little upset that Dipika wouldn't be able to make it, but she rejoiced when she heard about the surprise party. Mihir took her aside briefly to tell her that they would break the news of her pregnancy when Dipika arrived at the Radisson for brunch the next day. Then they would ask both Kartik and Dipika for permission to get engaged. They even planned to buy a diamond ring in the morning before brunch. Neither Ruhi nor Mihir wanted their engagement to be a grand affair, where hundreds of people turn up only to eat and half the time is spent acknowledging guests whom you've never seen before in your life. They wanted to keep it simple, a small gathering where the only people present would be those who actually loved and valued them.

After discussing these plans, Mihir and Ruhi joined the others. Once they were settled, they started drinking. Mihir had ordered pizzas for everyone and Kartik had made a playlist of Ruhi's favourite songs for the night. They danced and sang, and had loads of fun. Pooja left early, around ten o'clock, as her parents were strict. The others continued to enjoy themselves. Mihir could see that Ruhi was happy; it was visible in her eyes. Was it because they were actually taking their relationship forward? But she was drinking, and that worried Mihir, considering she was pregnant. He didn't want to say anything and upset her though.

When the cake was cut, Mihir applied a piece all over her face. She went to her room to clean it, and he followed her there. Once inside, he grabbed her and kissed her. He had been longing for it; the kiss still contained the same passion that it had a couple of years ago. After a while, when he thought they had had enough alcohol, he took Ruhi to her room and made her lie down. He looked at her face keenly for a few minutes; it still had the same innocence in it. Once she was asleep, he kissed her on her forehead and bid her goodbye. When he came out of Ruhi's room, Kartik was still drinking. Mihir put his glass away and took Kartik to his room to put him to bed. Once that was done, Mihir finally left for his home, full of excitement about the next day. In addition to the ring and the proposal, he had planned many surprises for Ruhi.

He was all set for a new beginning, leaving all the fights, grudges and bitterness in the past where they belonged. Little did he know everything would end before the fresh start. The sun never rose again for Ruhi. If only he knew that those would be his last moments with her, he would have held her tight, willing the universe to let her stay. It wasn't her time to go. But she was gone. He had always loved planning surprises for Ruhi, but in the end, life surprised him with her death.

~

'Do you want another cup of tea?' Inspector Kumawat asked Mihir, seeing the stress on his face. He had just finished his third cup.

'No, I just want to leave. Can I? I hope I've told you all that you need to know.' Mihir took a sip of water from the glass on the table in front of him.

'Not before you answer a few more questions,' Inspector Kumawat responded, noting something down in his file. After staring at the papers for a minute or two, he looked up again.

'Do you think that because you were going to reveal her pregnancy to both Kartik and Dipika the next day, she killed herself out of guilt? She wasn't ready to face them despite you being ready to accept her and take the relationship forward?'

'I don't know, Inspector. If the dead could talk, I would've known. It's not like I was going to reveal it against her will. We discussed it, and she agreed. If she wasn't ready, she should have at least told me. I wouldn't have taken that step.' Mihir looked depressed.

'One last question. Who was the person with whom she had an affair?' Inspector Kumawat asked, closing the case file.

Mihir shrugged. 'I don't know—I never bothered to find out. How would it have mattered to me? We had gotten over it; her promise never to see that person again was enough for me. Knowing his identity would have hurt me more. As for her family, even today, Dipika knows nothing about all this. Even today, she thinks that we were going to confess at brunch that it was my child and that was why we were planning to get engaged. At the end of the day, I loved Ruhi and I didn't want the child to suffer. I also didn't want her dignity to be questioned. I hope I have made everything clear.' He added, 'Also, please Inspector, it's a request ... don't try to pin this on any of the family members. We all loved her and would never even think about harming her. If you think it was a suicide, we are fine with that conclusion. We have lost her, and none of this will bring her back. But if you think someone killed her, then search for the person with whom she had the affair ... like you are searching for the stalker from Kartik's story. Who knows ... maybe they're the same person?'

'You can go now,' Inspector Kumawat said. He got up from his chair and shook hands with Mihir.

'Thank you, Inspector.' Mihir walked out, leaving Inspector Kumawat with conflicting thoughts on the case. They had closed the file, but questions still floated in the air. Who had been the father of the child? Was it really guilt that had driven Ruhi to kill herself? Did the stalker that Kartik claimed to have seen really exist, and if he did, was he the person with whom Ruhi had had an affair? Was it a suicide or had someone actually killed her on the night before her twenty-fifth birthday?

With all this uncertainty around the nature of her death, could Ruhi's soul rest in peace?

# chapter nine

*You think I would have killed myself? That I would just end my life and go far away from my loved ones who cared for me and would do anything to keep me happy? I had everything one could ask for: a caring brother, an affectionate sister and a loving boyfriend. You think I could take a step that would hurt Kartik so badly? You think I would just leave Mihir midway when we had decided to stay together for life? We were about to make our relationship official, and he was ready to shoulder the responsibilities of a father. I had everything Di, why would I kill myself? Please listen to your heart and believe what Kartik says.*

'No, this isn't possible,' Dipika shouted. Tushar rushed into her bedroom to see her thrashing about underneath the thick blanket, covered in sweat.

'Dipika, wake up,' Tushar said gently and shook her shoulder, moving a sweat-soaked curl from her forehead with his other hand. Her eyes snapped open and they were full of terror.

'It's okay ... shush ... it was just a dream.'

Tushar did his best to soothe her. His fingers ran through her hair and then brushed her cheek. Dipika was shaking as Tushar sat beside her and wrapped his arms around her. He could feel her relax as he pressed his face against her clammy skin.

'Please, stay with me,' she begged. Tushar sighed, tightening his grip around her. Tushar was exhausted. He had stayed awake the entire night with Dipika, who was burning with fever. The previous day, she had been interrogated again by Inspector Kumawat. He had asked her generic questions about Ruhi's mental state and behaviour in the days before her death. He also took her formal statement acknowledging the closing of the case, as there was still no evidence that pointed to a murder.

Since the interrogation, Dipika had been feeling weak and running a high temperature. Hence, Tushar was taking care of her. The case and investigation had taken a heavy toll on her health. Now she just wanted to put a full stop to it and return to a normal life.

'It wasn't just a dream,' she said. She leaned back in bed and drank the glass of water that Tushar gave her. 'I heard Ruhi's voice as if she was talking to me. The images were blurred, but I could clearly hear her say that she didn't kill herself and that I should believe what Kartik is saying.'

'You mean the stalker story?' Tushar asked, taking the glass from her.

'I don't know exactly what it meant but yeah … I guess so. It wasn't just a dream.' Dipika looked at him with swollen eyes.

'Dipika, it's just the fever that's giving you such weird thoughts. You haven't been well since yesterday ... and you're stressed because of the investigation. Look, I am an officer in the Gurgaon station; although I'm not handling the case, I keep myself updated on its progress. The police have not found any evidence to suggest that it wasn't suicide, and I think you should stop thinking too much about it.' Tushar got up from the bed and walked towards the table where he had kept a thermos bottle. He poured coffee from it into two cups. 'Also, Kartik is getting discharged tomorrow and he certainly wouldn't want to see you like this. He will think that I am incapable of caring for you and that I neglected your health all these months. You just can't spoil my image like this ...' Tushar said, trying to make her smile as he handed her a cup of coffee.

'Shut up.' She smiled, taking a sip. 'But you are right, I am overthinking things. It's just ... this headache is getting on my nerves. But I don't want Kartik to go through any stress after getting discharged. I want him to have a fresh start, a future full of happiness and laughter ...'

'That's right.'

If it hadn't been for Tushar, she would've had a breakdown too. From the day of Ruhi's death till now, he had been by her side, helping her regain her mental balance. It wasn't easy for him to switch roles from being a police officer at the station where the case was under investigation, to being the partner of one of the principal witnesses in the case. But he had managed it really well. There were moments when Dipika had lost her will to live and Tushar uplifted her; there were times when she missed Ruhi so terribly, and Tushar showered her with attention to redirect her focus to her own healing and well-being. He wanted her to be strong and face the reality, especially now that she had an added responsibility with Kartik getting discharged.

Dipika thanked Tushar for everything he had done for her and then, after a moment, said, 'You know ... I feel I shouldn't have taken that decision.'

'Which decision?' Tushar raised his eyebrows.

'That night ... I should have told them at work that I have to leave, that it was my sister's birthday party. But I put my work first.'

'It wouldn't have made any difference,' Tushar said.

'I don't know ... maybe if I had gone home, everything would be as it was. I still feel guilty.'

'Stop doing this to yourself. You have to understand that it wasn't in your control.'

Dipika knew there was sense in what Tushar was saying, but the thought still lingered in her mind. So often in life our most trivial acts or decisions lead to terrible consequences. We feel we shouldn't have done this or said that, at a certain time or in a particular place. But we can't stop things from happening. It's someone else that's controlling our life. And it doesn't matter whether you are up for it or not; if He has decided to change gears, He will.

~

Our lives are like unfinished works of art that need a retouch every now and then. Kartik had been recreating his own, and he hoped his release from the hospital would bring a new dawn in his life. Dipika was also feeling better now that her brother was returning home after seven months. She and Tushar were waiting for him outside the hospital on the morning of his discharge. Mihir was yet to join them, although he and Pooja were already on their way. He had promised Dipika that he would be there for Kartik.

When Dipika entered the hospital compound with Tushar, she saw her dad's car in the parking area. He was there to complete the discharge formalities, but the staff had asked him to wait. He accompanied Dipika and Tushar to the cafeteria for a cup of tea.

'When are you guys planning to get married?' her dad asked, just to make conversation. He was not in constant touch with Dipika, but he knew that they had been dating for a while.

Dipika, however, gave him a hostile look. She didn't want to answer the question, but finally gave in and replied, 'As of now, my priority is to be with Kartik. Tushar and I are not thinking of anything for the next couple of years at least. Kartik needs me, and I just cannot be selfish like you, leaving him to pursue my own happiness.'

'It's okay, uncle. She is right ... we have discussed it many times. We are both ready to wait.'

'You don't have to bring that up every time. I was generally asking ...' her dad retorted. 'I have asked you so many times to move back home, but you insist on keeping these grudges alive. At least now, when Kartik is about to start afresh, you can give this some thought. If you have lost a sister, I have lost my daughter. Even if she hated me for what happened, she was still my child.'

'No dad, I am not against you. I am sure even Kartik isn't,' Dipika clarified. 'But some distance will be good for all of us. Let's not interfere in each other's lives. What Kartik needs right now is a peaceful environment.'

'I am happy that you're there for each other. Please take care of her,' her dad said to Tushar. 'Also, if you need anything, don't hesitate to ask me.'

'Sure.' Tushar exchanged smiles with him.

Dipika couldn't react openheartedly, but she was happy that her dad had at least acknowledged her relationship.

'I may not be with you, but I have always cared for you and always will,' her dad added. He was interrupted by a hospital staff member who informed him that he was required to complete some paperwork. Mihir and Pooja had also arrived by then. Everyone made their way to the lobby to see Kartik standing on the other side of a glass door. Dipika couldn't control her tears; every time she had visited him in the past few months, she had been emotional. He looked weak and his happy demeanour was gone. She kept looking at him, wanting to hug him and give him the strength he needed.

I promise to clean up all the cuts and wounds of your life. I will bandage up the memories and dry your tears. I won't let them weigh you down anymore. I will lift all that weight off of you, so you don't have to be haunted anymore. I will lift you up and hold your hand when you stumble. A piece of your heart will always be a part of mine, and that makes me happy. I'll always be someone you can count on ... someone who'll never let you feel alone. As long as you have me, you'll never feel unloved.

Kartik went into Dr Singh's office for one last time. He was gazing at every corner of the room; he had spent so much time there in the past seven months. It felt like home now. He had always wanted to run from there and escape as he often felt caged during the sessions. But today, on the day he was finally free, he just wanted to lock himself in; he was scared to face the world outside. It felt like memories of Ruhi, whom he missed every minute of every day, lingered in that room.

'All the best for your future life.' Dr Singh smiled.

'I hope to never see you again, Dr Singh. But I thank you for everything.' Kartik shook hands with him before leaving.

All the discharge formalities were done. A new life had opened its doors to him. It was time to start on a journey to the find the joy he had lost, although now it felt like it would take forever. Hopefully, he would smile again.

~

There are so many things in life that you can't hold on to. Love happens to be one of those. When you love someone, you want that person to stay in your life forever. You are convinced that, without them, existence would just be a black hole. Some survive, some suffer; in both cases, life moves on. For some, it's just a matter of time, and for others, it's a lifetime. For Kartik, it was a long wait, as if time had just stopped. It was June and temperatures were soaring in Delhi. At least, Kartik felt it was hot, but it had been a long time since he had stepped outside. He wasn't even sure what normal weather felt like anymore. After greeting everyone briefly, Kartik and Dipika left with their father, who had insisted on dropping them home. They rode in silence for several minutes. Kartik gazed at the roads and the cars outside; it felt like everything was moving fast, except him.

*What's my daily routine going to be like*, he wondered, as they entered the lane of the apartment where Dipika had shifted after Ruhi's death. Each day in the hospital had been identical to the next—the same routine of getting up, exercising, appointments with doctors, reading and taking rest. Suddenly, this new freedom seemed like a hallucination.

After a few minutes, his dad spoke, looking at them in the rear view mirror. 'It's fine if you both want to be left alone, but please, if you need anything, do call me. I know you don't want me to interfere in your lives, but Kartik has just come out of the hospital, and keeping tabs on his health is important, even when you're in office,' he said to Dipika.

'I have already taken leave for a week. But thanks for being here for us today,' she responded.

'Thank you for coming, Dad,' Kartik added.

Was it the loneliness inside that hospital which made him value the people in his life more? It was unusual of him to thank his dad for anything. Some things in life are learnt only with experience. His dad smiled as he dropped them in front of the apartment. Kartik observed his new surroundings carefully. The lane had more than a dozen buildings, all similar to each other; he looked at their apartment building keenly. It reminded him of how they all used to live together under one roof—Ruhi, Dipika and him. He could still hear Ruhi calling out to him every now and then; he could picture her smiling and walking cheerfully around their home. Dipika held his hand as she could sense what was going on in his mind. She looked at him and tightened her grip on his hand to signal that she was there for him. Kartik smiled reluctantly and walked up to the gate with his bag.

'Welcome back. I have missed you terribly these past months. It wasn't easy.' Dipika's happiness was evident on her face.

'It wasn't easy for me either. It still isn't. I was desperate to be back with you and the others. But now that I'm out, I feel there's something missing. Something is not right. I don't know what it is but I am unable to get rid of this feeling. It's not that I am still feeling depressed like I used to, but something is haunting me,' Kartik tried to explain as they walked in through the gate.

Dipika handed him a note that she had written for him, and made him read it before they entered the apartment. She had scribbled it the previous night when she couldn't sleep. She had wanted time to pass quickly so Kartik could be home as soon as possible. Since this morning, she had been preparing all the little things he loved. She wasn't an expert writer, but Kartik smiled as he read the note, and the return of that smile meant everything to her.

*When you're sad and depressed, I'll be here to put a smile on your face. When you're angry and frustrated, I'll be here to calm you down. You'll never feel alone because when you're hurt and in tears, I'll wipe them away. When there is something on your mind that you need to express, I'll be here to listen and understand and to believe what you say. Don't be confused; we'll figure out things together. Now that you are back, I promise I'll be your strength, and if you feel scared, I'll be here to protect you. I will stand by you through thick and thin because there's no-buddy like you, my brother.*

Kartik hugged her the moment he finished reading the note. The volcano of tears that was concealed inside him erupted. All these months, he had suppressed his feelings, not letting them explode. Now, he let out all those emotions that had been killing him slowly since the day Ruhi died. When his soul soaked in those soothing words, he couldn't control himself anymore. Dipika too had tear-filled eyes, but she had to be strong for him and didn't break down while letting him cry. They didn't really need anyone else as long as they had each other. Kartik knew Dipika would be his greatest support in the days to come; he respected her from the bottom of his heart. She knew her role so well and was standing next to him, rock solid. Wherever Ruhi was, he thought, she would be smiling at the sight of them together, standing strong and ready to face whatever life had in store for them.

The welcome wasn't over yet. Dipika wanted Kartik to feel loved, so she had planned things accordingly. The minute Kartik walked in through the door, he saw that the entire house was decorated with pretty welcome-themed balloons and ribbons. Kartik hadn't anticipated anything of this sort; he was speechless. It made him feel really special and he couldn't thank Dipika enough. And when he thought it was all done, there they were—Mihir, Pooja and Tushar. They had reached before Kartik and Dipika, and were waiting for them; it was part of the surprise. When you have such people in your life, your problems look smaller, even if they don't entirely disappear. Nothing could compare with these precious moments with loved ones. Kartik was smiling again. He felt like he had spent decades away from these people who were his family. When Dipika went into the kitchen along with Mihir and Pooja, he sat down with Tushar.

'I don't know how to thank you for being there for my sister. She told me how you've supported her these past months. I'm sure it wasn't easy for you, given your job ...' Kartik began.

'If I have duties towards my department, then I have my duty towards her too. We are happy that you are finally back, Kartik. Now she will feel a little relaxed. There wasn't a day when she didn't remember you.' Tushar avoided mentioning Ruhi as he didn't want to evoke painful memories.

'You know, I didn't really trust you when we first met. I mean, I thought police officers were rude ... that they don't have emotions. But I was wrong.' Kartik smiled.

Tushar laughed and said, 'I'm glad. Or she would have left me by now. But we are trained to be that way on the job. Can't really help it.'

The others came out of the kitchen then, carrying his favourite dishes, including a large pizza and coke. Mihir had ordered his friend's favourite pizza, knowing he wouldn't have tasted it for months. Kartik had missed Mihir terribly. He knew Mihir must have suffered equally, as he loved Ruhi. Seeing him smile made him feel better. He must have eventually realised that he needed to move on, keeping the happy memories alive. Meeting everyone after such a long time relaxed Kartik's mind. All these months, he had feared that Dipika wouldn't love him the way she used to. He even had nightmares about Mihir and Pooja avoiding him so as not to relive the memories of Ruhi's death. But he could see now that nothing had changed.

Once they had their share of pizza, Mihir went to the balcony for a smoke and Kartik followed.

'I'm not going to let you smoke,' Mihir said.

'I don't want to. I just came to say that I am much better now, and with all of you by my side, I feel positive about the future.'

'Of course. You are back and smiling. What more do we want?' Mihir gave him a friendly hug and added, 'I need to talk to you about something. Not now, but maybe tomorrow we could catch up somewhere. A lot has happened and I want you to know about it.'

Pooja joined them on the balcony and said to Kartik, 'It's so good to see you both like this. Initially, I thought Mihir would give you company inside the hospital, seeing how badly he was missing you. But I'm glad that didn't happen. If it had, I doubt you both would have ever wanted to come out,' she bantered.

'That would have been a good move, actually. The doctors would have thrown us out long ago.' Mihir laughed.

Kartik grinned; he had never thought that his homecoming would bring such contentment, and that distance would only bring him closer to his loved ones. The seasons had changed, but their relationships had endured. In their hearts, Ruhi was still alive, and her enduring memories had created a magnetic force that only pulled them closer together. They were like the branches of a tree; they had grown in different directions over the past few months, but remained connected to each other against all odds.

~

'Are we ever going to talk about it?' Kartik asked softly once everyone had left. He was sitting with Dipika who had just switched the television to Netflix.

'I thought you would want to watch something after a long time,' Dipika replied, switching the TV off.

'I would have. But you know what I'm talking about. Don't you? We have refrained from discussing it all day. But I ought to know why it was hidden from me.'

'You mean Ruhi's pregnancy?' Dipika asked, sitting upright on the sofa. Kartik nodded and she continued, 'What was I supposed to tell you? And what could you have done with that piece of information? The doctors had suggested not disclosing it at that time as it would have probably made your condition worse. They didn't want to take the risk; I am not an expert, so I had no choice but to follow their advice. Why would I risk stressing you out by revealing a piece of information that wouldn't have helped in any way?'

'I had the right to know.' There was a sadness on Kartik's face.

'I am not denying that. I am just saying that some things should be revealed only at the right time; it's important to analyse the situation before disclosing such news. I had a brief discussion with Mihir after I was informed by the police. I was as shocked by the news as you are now. Mihir said they were planning to tell us during brunch on Ruhi's birthday, along with the news that they were going to make their relationship official. They just needed a few days to prepare themselves. He thought her birthday would be the perfect time.'

Kartik was partially convinced. What Dipika was saying made sense, he had to admit. He shifted on the sofa and said, 'Mihir has asked me to meet him tomorrow. He said we need to talk. Maybe he wants to clear all this up.'

'Or maybe not,' Dipika said.

Dipika's words made Kartik anxious. What did she mean by that? Did she already know what Mihir wanted to talk about? And if it wasn't about Ruhi's pregnancy, then what did he want to disclose? The suspense was already making him edgy.

# chapter ten

It wasn't an easy night for Kartik. The new bedroom felt unfamiliar; he had gotten rather used to his hospital bed. Despite his new freedom, he felt trapped. His mind wandered. Unable to sleep, he got up and paced restlessly from one room to another. For a while, he looked at himself in the mirror; his face wasn't the same as before. He went back to bed and closed his eyes, but his thoughts kept him awake.

Once Kartik even looked out of his bedroom window, hoping to catch a glimpse of the stalker. But no one was around. The streets lay empty under the moonlight. Even so, he couldn't find an escape route from his persistent thoughts. Everyone had tried so hard to make him feel at home, yet the very air in his room felt strange. The doctors had told him that it would take time to get used to a normal life in his new environment, but what continued to trouble him were the familiar echoes that had haunted him all these months. He wanted to be free of them and had worked hard to compose himself, but peace still eluded him.

When the first rays of light fell on his face, he realised that he had struggled with himself the entire night. After freshening up, he sat down for breakfast, made by Dipika. She knew he was going to meet Mihir that morning and hoped that he wouldn't stress himself over it. The doctors had advised maintaining a peaceful and healthy environment around him, and she didn't want it to be disturbed.

'I'll drop you on the way to office,' Dipika said, handing him a glass of juice. 'Make sure that you come back home and relax after meeting Mihir. I could hear you walking about last night; you hardly slept. You need rest, Kartik.'

'I'm fine. I'll take care,' Kartik said, faking a smile as he didn't want her to get worried.

Dipika dropped him at Cyber Hub where he was supposed to meet Mihir. Every step he took towards it reminded him of all the moments he had spent with Ruhi and Dipika there. They used to love spending time there. There wasn't a place in the city that did not hold memories of Ruhi for him. At the café, Kartik was about to call Mihir when he walked in. After ordering two cups of coffee, Mihir was silent for a while. He didn't know where to begin. He didn't want to start the conversation in a way that would hurt Kartik. It wasn't easy for Mihir to talk about his feelings and his life after Ruhi's death either. He wasn't even sure if it was the right time to speak about these things, but he had to. Kartik was his best friend, and he had promised Dipika and Tushar he would have this talk with him once he was discharged. He could no longer just hang out with him and keep his feelings trapped inside, he decided. After taking a deep breath, he broke the silence softly.

'I need to tell you something. Maybe I've delayed it too long. Dipika might have told you about it, but I feel I should personally clarify things. I don't want you to get the wrong impression.'

Kartik was expecting him to talk about Ruhi's pregnancy. Dr Singh had disclosed it, and he had discussed it with Dipika the previous night, but he wanted to hear it from Mihir. He was still hurt by the fact that everyone had concealed the truth from him.

'I don't need to tell you how difficult it was to go through it all. It happened all of a sudden, and we could do nothing. For an entire month, I was mourning her death and hardly even stepped out of my house. I don't know what it was—guilt or the pain of losing her. We all felt guilty ... even Dipika felt guilty for not being there, and you had your own reasons. Each of us felt that we could've saved her, but the truth is that we can't change fate. I knew it was beyond my control, but still I felt responsible. The suffering went on for months. Dipika was in her own world ... it wasn't that we didn't interact, but we met less frequently. So many times I felt like calling her, but I couldn't. There was a strange awkwardness between all of us.'

'What are you trying to say?' Kartik interrupted, puzzled as to where this conversation was going.

'I'm coming to the point,' Mihir said, and continued to describe what he had been through. 'I was aware that moving on is a process of healing your heart. I knew that I could, and eventually would, move on. But the problem was ... I just didn't know when or how. There were times I thought I had finally moved on, but then, I would realise I had failed. I started feeling that losing was a game that I had mastered, and I won each and every time. People say that it gets better, that the pain goes away. I told myself I just need to keep pushing and live from one day to the next. But I couldn't let go and leave her behind. I was afraid that if I did ... she would be nothing more than a memory. As time passed, I realised that every person we love is going to hurt or leave us, but sometimes we end up finding a person who heals us.'

Mihir paused for a second to sip his coffee. Kartik was staring at him. It dawned on him that his friend wasn't talking about his sister's pregnancy. It was about something else.

'During that period, when I was heartbroken and lonely, Pooja healed me. Despite her own grief, she helped me to get over mine. I don't know if it was the need for emotional support that drew us closer, or if we served as escape routes for each other to move on, but I felt alive again. We became each other's strength. You know, out of nowhere comes that ray of hope. She was the one who gave me that hope, and probably in my company, she felt the same.'

'So?' Though he was beginning to comprehend what his friend wanted to tell him, Kartik was still unsure.

'It's been a couple of months … we are in a relationship. We didn't realise it for a long time, that we had developed feelings for each other. We couldn't even understand if it was right or wrong, but the storm inside our hearts had settled and we just went with the flow. I wanted you to be the first to know, but Dr Singh wouldn't allow it. I don't know how you feel about this. Maybe you'll take time to accept it, and I am okay with that. Even I took my time to make peace with my feelings. If you can't digest it right away, I understand. But I can't move on happily without letting my best friend know about it—not after all that we've gone through together.'

Kartik's face was expressionless. He didn't know what he was supposed to say. He had lost his sister, but that was no reason to stop someone else from moving on with their life. In fact, if Ruhi hadn't been his sister, he would probably have advised Mihir to move on, just as everyone around him was insisting that he move on as well. The heart is like a key; it keeps getting resized for the next lock. Sometimes it goes deep into the lock before realising it's not a match. It keeps getting reshaped with each attempt until it finds the right lock. The day your key fits and you know it's a match, you experience that feeling which people refer to when they say, 'When you know, you know'. But what if you find the match, the lock that you are meant to open, but while turning the key something goes wrong? The key has to reshape itself again and find another lock to open. Mihir's heart had found that lock in Pooja's.

Kartik had no clue how to react to his friend's revelation. Should he be happy for his friend who had finally moved on after a long struggle with grief, or be sad for his beloved sister who was no longer in this world?

'I am happy for you,' Kartik said finally, in a somewhat subdued tone, 'but I am also hurt.'

'Look, it's not that I have forgotten Ruhi; her memories will always be with me,' Mihir said, anxious to justify himself.

'I'm not talking about that. I thought you wanted to tell me your version of Ruhi's pregnancy.'

Mihir sighed; he had known that was coming. 'I wanted to, but I thought Dipika might have talked to you about it. She mentioned that Dr Singh informed you about it.'

'Yes, he did, but I expected that the people close to me would tell me first, no matter what the situation was,' Kartik reiterated firmly.

On his insistence, Mihir narrated the entire story of the affair Ruhi had, which culminated in her pregnancy. He also told Kartik that, after the police, he was the first to know about the affair; he hadn't even revealed it to Dipika yet. Kartik was taken aback. He couldn't believe his ears. His heart pounded and he felt he was drowning in the depths of a new, terrifying reality. It was as if a fire was burning deep inside him, and he wanted to shut himself out from the world, for everything felt unreal.

*Ruhi couldn't have had an affair ... she truly loved Mihir. If something like that had been going on, she wouldn't have hidden it from me. It's not the truth. It can't be. I always saw unconditional love in her eyes when she looked at Mihir. This couldn't be the reason she ended her life. The case may be closed, but I'll dig the truth out from the deepest grave. If I can bring myself to believe Mihir's story, was the guy who was hanging around that night her boyfriend? Were they arguing over her pregnancy? What was it all about? Fuck, this can't be true.*

'I was ready to resume the relationship despite knowing about the affair. And she was happy about it. I don't know what was going through her mind when she decided to kill herself,' Mihir concluded.

'Are you kidding me? Have you gone nuts? You know how much she loved you. She would have done anything for you, and here you are, saying that she told you the child wasn't yours. How could you believe something like that? Did you do a DNA test to verify? She was lying to you. I'm telling you ... I saw her arguing with someone that evening. Did you try to find out what she was hiding and for what reasons?'

'Kartik, I read messages on her phone from a person who was saying that he wouldn't hurt her like I did. Promising he wouldn't fight with her like I used to. Do you think after seeing all that, not to mention the change in her behaviour, I would have doubted what she confessed?'

'Yes, because it wasn't the truth. It had to be your child. She didn't kill herself. And now that you have revealed all this, I am sure she was hiding something from all of us because she was under pressure. He made her do it, that stalker.'

Kartik was angry. Was everyone around him blind, or were they just running away from reality? However, he was forced to remind himself that everyone had a right to their own opinion. Where would he look for the courage to find his voice, to tell the true story of Ruhi's death? Was it too late, or did he still have a chance? Was he destined to be silent, emotionally irresolute and unable to access the truth? With so many versions of the story around, would he be able to separate lies from truth? Or would he succumb to his own perceptions that had blinded him all these months? Only time would tell.

~

*Have you ever felt as if your soul was out of place? Like your existence is nothing but a disgrace. Where you are reaching for a future you're not ready to face, living a life that you don't even want to embrace. Lost in reality's futile race, you feel like a toy that's out of place. Everything around you is moving too fast and you can't keep up with the pace. Swallowed by an internal darkness, you're no longer able to interpret what's real and what's fiction, what's the truth and what's a lie.*

Every emotion that Kartik was going through opened a Pandora's box of possibilities that increased the confusion in his mind. After his conversation with

Mihir, he hovered like a lost soul around the city till evening. Then, instead of going back home, his feet led him towards one of the local bars. The voice of his soul begged him not to go, but another voice urged him to hurry. A fire was burning inside him and this was the only way to douse the flames.

'Two bottles of beer,' he said to the waiter as he sat down at a corner table. The place looked shady. All the other tables were occupied by locals; a few were sitting alone like him. He wondered if they were also going through the kind of trauma that he had experienced today. Looking down at the screen of his phone, he saw the date: 29 June.

*Seven months*, Kartik realised. The thought made him feel even more fragile. He knew he was suffering an emotional breakdown again. He tried hard to stop himself from drinking, but couldn't. He poured himself a mug of beer from the bottle in front of him and gulped it down in one go. A pleasant chill spread through his entire body, bringing him relief. It had been seven months since he'd had a drink. With each sip of beer, he recollected that night. Images of Ruhi jumping in joy when she heard about her surprise party, and of Ruhi, Mihir and Pooja having a gala time, flashed through his mind. Suddenly, he had a blackout, like the one he had had that night. When his vision returned, he pictured Ruhi lying on the floor, dead. He downed one drink after another, with the hope that the alcohol would help him remember exactly what had happened.

*I'll be as free as a bird from now on; no worries, no tensions, nothing.* The voice still echoed in his head, but he still couldn't visualise the person it belonged to. He continued drinking despite Dr Singh's warning to stay away from alcohol. He no longer cared; after all those months in hospital, he was still the same. The treatment was useless, he thought; at least this might help. Another drink, and Mihir's words from their conversation that morning came floating back: he has moved on, she was having an affair and it wasn't his child. That gave him a sudden jolt and he messaged Dipika.

*Why do you have to do this? It was fine to do it once, but you still kept half the truth to yourself. You think I will not be able to handle it. You're wrong; by doing this, you've made me fall into the trap again. I now know what you meant by saying 'maybe not' yesterday. You could have told me. How could you believe that she'd had an affair? You knew Ruhi better than me, right? Yet she was hiding something from all of us. You, me, Mihir—everyone. I don't want to talk to you anymore. Step by step, you are breaking me by trying to protect me.*

As he paid the bill and got up, his head spun; he was drunk. Regaining his balance somehow, he made his way out of the bar. It was very dark. There were only a few cars on the street. Kartik could hardly walk, but managed somehow. Seven months, and the pain was still fresh. He wanted to scream with all his strength, telling the entire city that Ruhi didn't have an affair. She was innocent. He wanted to prove it, but couldn't find a way. He wanted to know what had forced her to lie about it. He wished she was alive; he would've made her believe that she didn't need to worry about anything and that her brother would always stand by her. Tears rolled down his cheeks. As he was wiping them, a Bullet rode past. The rider's helmet visor was open, and for a second, he turned his head towards Kartik, giving him goose bumps. It was him: the figure from his nightmares, the one whose image had tormented him all these months.

'Stop!' Kartik shouted as loudly as he could.

The bike stopped a few metres away from him. The rider looked at him for a moment through the rear-view mirror of the bike. In the headlights of a passing car, Kartik could see his long hair. Yes, it was him—the stalker. The man no one believed even existed was right in front of him. Kartik screamed again as he staggered forward; he wanted to drag him off the bike and cut him into pieces. But the bike disappeared into the darkness of the night. Kartik cursed himself for failing to note down the licence plate number. For months, everyone had tried to convince him that it was only a hallucination. But there he was, in the flesh; the stalker from his story was real.

~

*Remember, I told you that you are just a character in my story. I am the one who's writing your life. I warned you that your mind is your demon, denying the truth that is right in front of you. But I'll make you believe in me. Your mind kept telling you that all this was a hallucination but I, time after time, advised you to listen to me—your soul. Your inner voice tried to unmask the hidden truth countless times, but you always listened to the other voices instead. All I ever wanted was to calm your crowded mind. But you always assumed that your intellect was superior to your instincts and emotions. Your mind kept telling you that you were trapped in an illusion because there was no concrete evidence to justify your feelings. I cannot prove anything to anyone. You simply have to believe in my power. So many times you have done something that everyone else felt was wrong. And you turned out to be right. I made that possible because you kept your faith in me on those occasions. But this time, my power had slowly faded, quenching the flames in your heart. You did feel the absence of warmth, didn't you? Now that I have made you feel my existence again, I'll show you the power that I hold. For your own good. Illness, nausea, grief ... let it all go. Know your soul, your trapped soul, because your brain will die. But I, your soul, am immortal.*

## chapter eleven

How often do we talk about letting go and crib that it isn't easy? How easy is it for trees to shed their old leaves? Do they regret every leaf that changes over time and falls? Or do they let go of them naturally, relishing the weightlessness because it was meant to be? Dipika had kept herself strong when the storm was at its worst, but now, her very core was weakened by the sight of Kartik breaking down all over again.

The police had informed her about Mihir's statement regarding Ruhi's affair before Kartik's discharge. She had withheld this information from her brother with the best of intentions. There was no point in opening old wounds, she felt. And in the end, that was exactly what had happened. Kartik, after returning home late and totally drunk the previous night, was still sleeping in his room.

She had no way to convince Kartik not to look back. It wasn't that she didn't regret what had happened to her sister. But she wanted to handle things maturely. She knew it wasn't the kind of high-profile case that the police would give priority to; in fact, they had already closed it. Dipika didn't have the money or political contacts to fight the system. She was an ordinary middle-class working girl who had always been taught to accept things she could not change—be it her father's behaviour or Ruhi's death. Moreover, in a relentless hunt for the truth, she didn't want to lose the few loved ones who remained in her life.

Tushar had come by in the morning as Dipika was extremely upset. She told him, 'He was all over the place last night, talking utter nonsense. First he messaged me, and when he got home, he had no control over himself. He blamed me and everyone else, and said all kinds of things. What should I do? I don't know how to tell him that such behaviour is only damaging his health further.' Dipika was almost in tears. She couldn't bear to see her brother walking on the path of self-destruction.

'You have to give him time. You knew this would happen once Mihir revealed it all. Perhaps it was necessary for Kartik to let it all out. At least he is not keeping it all bottled up like he used to.' Tushar was aware that Kartik's behaviour last night was cause for concern, but he tried to present it in a positive light for Dipika's sake.

'You are justifying his drinking? The doctors have warned him to stay away from alcohol as he is still on heavy medication and it could have adverse effects and lead to a breakdown.'

Tushar came closer to Dipika and put his hand on her shoulder. 'I am not saying it was right. But if we keep nagging him, he'll stop discussing things with us. I don't want that to happen.'

'I had a word with Mihir yesterday; he called after meeting Kartik at the restaurant. He said that Kartik was yelling that Ruhi didn't have an affair and that the child wasn't someone else's. He believes she was hiding something because she was under some kind of pressure. More than the news of Mihir and Pooja's relationship, he completely lost his cool when he heard about Ruhi's secret.'

'I don't know what makes him feel that way. Maybe it's his stalker theory,' Tushar reflected.

'He says he saw him yesterday,' Dipika revealed.

'The stalker?'

'Yes. He told me after coming home drunk last night that he saw him outside Cyber Hub on a Bullet.'

Tushar was taken aback. 'It's all in his mind. Maybe the alcohol is making him visualise things that he's thinking about round the clock. Let me talk to him once he gets up. I'll try to make him understand.'

Dipika sighed. She was worried that Kartik would go back to square one after months of treatment. All she wanted was for him to be well again. The past few hours had been terribly depressing for her. Tushar pulled her close and she leaned on his chest. Nobody could have handled Dipika better in such situations. The maturity with which Tushar reacted to any kind of crisis in her life had made her fall more deeply in love with him. Whenever he was with her, all her worries disappeared.

Just his assurance that everything would be okay made her calmer. He made the most adverse circumstances look normal. Dipika wanted to say so many things to Tushar, but she didn't know how to thank or repay him for the peace and happiness he had brought her. He was her strength and her faith, and everything she had been looking for. Every day, she loved him more.

He got her something to eat from the kitchen; she hadn't eaten since last night with all the anxiety that had captured her mind. Even now, she was refusing to eat, but he insisted, feeding her with his own hands. She loved the way he pampered her when she was feeling low, never failing to bring a smile to her face. Isn't that a heavenly feeling? Love isn't about sweet talk; it's about being with each other when needed the most, and bringing each other comfort and peace when together. Tushar was a perfect match for Dipika in every sense, and she knew that her life wouldn't be complete without him.

He kissed her on the forehead as she ate her food. Just then, Kartik walked in. He was terribly hungover and felt like someone was banging his head. But he could remember every bit of the previous night, unlike the one that eluded his memory. The image of the stalker passing on a bike was vivid, as if he was still in front of his eyes. Did the stalker speed away because he realised who Kartik was, or was it just a coincidence, Kartik wondered. Deep in thought, he walked into the dining room and saw Tushar and Dipika in each other's arms.

'Sorry to disturb you guys.' He was instantly apologetic.

Dipika immediately released herself from Tushar's arms and adjusted her clothes awkwardly. Tushar made Kartik sit down and offered him some food.

'What made you drink yesterday?' Tushar asked, giving him a glass of lemonade. 'If you were stressed about something, you could have told us.'

Kartik didn't react; he took a sip of the lemonade and held his aching head in his hands. He was clearly not interested in having this conversation.

'You think we can't handle you?' Dipika couldn't help asking.

'It's not about handling, it's about believing. I saw Ruhi's stalker again last night. Yes, I was drunk, but I wasn't totally out of my senses. It was him, I'm certain.' Kartik was already raising his voice.

'I believe you,' Tushar assured him. 'So you saw him riding a Bullet last night outside Cyber Hub, right?'

'Yes. It was the same person I had seen arguing with Ruhi that evening. And outside the house later that night, from my window. I'd seen him hanging around a few times before that.'

'What was the licence plate number?' Tushar asked. 'I'll get one of my colleagues to track the owner of the bike. Unofficially, as the case is closed.'

'I couldn't see the number. It was dark. I only saw that it was a black Bullet.'

It saddened Kartik immensely. If only he had been able to get a glimpse of that number. Tushar was even offering to trace the guy, but without the licence plate, he had nothing to go on.

'Now, that's impossible. How are we supposed to search for him with absolutely no information? There are so many black Bullets in the city. We can't just go and haul up all the owners.'

'Why don't you check the CCTV cameras around that area? If we can get hold of the footage, I'll easily be able to recognise him.'

'We are not authorised to do that. This isn't some daily soap where anyone can get the footage of the highways without permission. I can only help you unofficially, and I'll see what I can do. But you need to do as I say. First, you need to trust me. Second, give me time. Also, I want you to update me if you remember anything.'

*I am such a fucking idiot. How could I miss something as important as the licence plate? If I had noted it down, Tushar could have helped me. But I am not going to spare him; by hook or by crook, I'll find him and expose his motive for killing Ruhi.*

Kartik cursed himself again and again, but never wavered from the certainty that it was the stalker who had murdered his sister.

'Kartik, how can you think I don't trust you or that I don't feel the pain of Ruhi's death,' Dipika said. 'But, at this moment, if I have a priority, it's you and your health. I have to live without Ruhi for the rest of my life, and I have accepted that reality. But I've had a hard time living through the past few months without you, and I don't want that to continue. I won't be able to accept that.'

'Don't worry, I'm fine. I was just upset that you believed Ruhi had an affair with someone else. She didn't. We have to find out what made her say so. Who was pressurising her so much that she had to lie even to Mihir, the father of her child?'

Dipika and Tushar tried their best to console him and eventually calmed him down. Kartik was confident, now that the stalker's existence was proven, that he would track him down and make his life hell.

~

After spending some time with them, Tushar left, wondering how he could sort things out. He got in his car, drove a few blocks ahead, found a parking spot and stopped. With a deep breath, he took his phone out of his pocket and scrolled down his contact list. He stared at a name on the screen for a few seconds before clicking on the call icon. After a few rings, the call was disconnected by the other person. Tushar tried calling again, and finally someone picked up.

'Are you in your senses? Can we have a word?' Tushar sounded annoyed.

'Tushar?' the other person responded. 'What happened?'

'What happened? As if you don't know and you didn't see him? He saw you yesterday, Shishir; he saw you outside Cyber Hub!' Tushar yelled at him.

'Shit, shit, I was going to call you about that.' Shishir sounded panic-stricken.

'Why the hell are you back in the city? You told me that you have shifted permanently, so what the fuck brings you to Gurgaon?' Tushar was furious.

'Please tell me what has happened ... please.' The fear in Shishir's voice was evident.

Tushar could hear another call coming in, and he removed the phone from his ear to check who it was. *Kartik* ... the name flashed on the screen. Why was he calling? Did he know something? Did he suddenly remember something about Shishir? Tushar toyed with the idea of picking up the call but decided to ignore it.

'Tushar ... are you there?'

'Yes. Kartik claims that he saw you last night. First, I want you to explain to me what you're doing in town. Second, why didn't you tell me, and why the heck did you have to stop when he yelled at you?'

'I didn't know it was him. I thought it was some random person calling out for help. When I looked in the mirror, I realised it was Kartik and I sped away.'

'Too late. He had already recognised you by then. Why did you have to come back here? No one had seen you; Kartik had almost started believing what everyone was telling him, that the stalker doesn't exist. The police have no evidence of you; everything was in place. But you just had to mess it up.'

'You told me the case was closed. I got a good opportunity here and didn't want to miss it.'

'You could've at least told me. All this while I have shielded you … and now you want to act like nothing has happened. Thankfully, he didn't get hold of your licence plate number. If he had, things would have been out of my hands.'

There was silence on the other end of the line. Shishir had realised his blunder. Tushar had protected him all this while, and he had almost given himself away. He had goosebumps when he asked, 'What should I do now?'

'Leave as soon as possible.' Tushar's reply sounded more like an order than a suggestion.

'Now? I can't leave for at least a week. I have to give my company notice. I've just signed on for a project here; I can't back out so suddenly,' Shishir said.

'One week, that's it. I'll manage till then somehow. Don't be afraid. Nothing's going to go wrong,' Tushar said coolly and disconnected the call.

## chapter twelve

Nobody really knows your struggles as you go through life. Part of the reality of life is hardship. That's not a negative statement; it's simply a statement of fact. Accepting that life is difficult makes it easier to deal with hard times. However, having a support system eases hardships. For Mihir, that support system was Pooja. Amidst the pain that had followed Ruhi's death, Pooja had become his solace. And he had promised to love her for the rest of his life. Mihir had had to become quite the emotional multitasker since Kartik's release from the hospital. He had to sustain a new and passionate relationship, while helping his best friend and dead girlfriend's brother to readjust to normal life. On the one hand, he was putting all his energy into supporting Kartik's recovery; on the other, he was endeavouring to give his undivided attention to Pooja.

One night, leaving behind all their worries for a few hours, he went on a dinner date with her to Downtown Café in Sector 29. It had been a while since they had actually gone out like a normal couple. Thankfully, they were both mature enough to realise that their relationship had begun in unusual circumstances. Wanting to make the evening special for Pooja, Mihir had booked a table at her favourite café in the city and ordered her favourite dishes. As they sat together, Pooja kept blushing at the way Mihir was looking at her. Without saying a word, he was telling her that something special was in store for her. They held hands with their fingers intertwined, and eventually, he broke the silence.

'You say that I am the best thing that ever happened to you. But you know what I feel? If it wasn't for your love, I don't know what my life would have become. You accepted me the way I was, knowing everything about my relationship with Ruhi. You literally pulled me out of the well I was drowning myself in.'

'It was only because I felt you are genuine.' Pooja smiled and added teasingly, 'You rarely find such boys these days.'

'That's quite an unfair statement. There are many, if you actually look out for them ... but the problem is you girls fall for the bad boys easily. Boys like me hardly even get a chance to express our feelings.' Mihir laughed.

'Oh please, don't be a lawyer here,' Pooja said with a grin.

The food was served and the smiles on their faces added spice to it. Mihir was content that he had found someone who could be his support and strength through life's ups and downs, and Pooja was happy to be with someone whose love was so genuine and heartfelt. Even though they didn't meet often, they felt each other's presence in their lives, and that was all that mattered. Even when he was far away, all she needed to feel better was a memory they had shared, or sometimes just a flower or a heartfelt note. This time he had got a huge bouquet of lovely flowers that he had left at the counter. Once their dinner was finished and the bill was paid, the manager presented the bouquet to Pooja. She couldn't stop blushing and her eyes reflected pure love. These little gestures always made her feel special; all she craved was his attention. The bouquet had a note attached to it; she opened it to read, *I love you, idiot.*

'I love you too.' Pooja grinned as Mihir helped her carry the bouquet.

As they walked out of the café, hand in hand, their faces glowed; love was all they could feel. With each step towards the parking lot, they felt the adrenaline rush, that urge to be closer to each other. It felt like it had been years since they had last made love, and they knew it was the moment now.

As they adjusted themselves in the car, Mihir said awkwardly, 'Can I turn the air-conditioning on? It's hot in here.'

'That's because I'm here,' Pooja said with a wink as she moved a little closer.

'That may be, but it's still too hot for me,' Mihir replied cheekily.

'Maybe you can't handle me, then,' Pooja retorted.

'On the contrary, the only thing I want to do is

handle you,' he said in a low voice, causing her cheeks to turn red again.

'Come here.' She grabbed his collar and pulled him over the gear box. In a moment, both had closed their eyes and, after a few seconds, when their lips were almost touching, Mihir opened his eyes slightly to look into hers. He wanted to savour the moment and see the passion in her eyes as they kissed. But the minute he opened his eyes, he was taken aback. He pushed her away and sat back in his seat. Ruhi's face had flashed in front of his eyes, and it wasn't happening for the first time. Every time he tried to get close to Pooja, Ruhi's face haunted him as if she were still alive. He just couldn't get her out of his mind, no matter how hard he tried. He was trembling and covered in goosebumps. Mihir had absolutely no clue why this kept happening when he had convinced himself that he had moved on. Yet, he couldn't control his thoughts or the way his body reacted. The fact that Pooja knew and understood it all, however, calmed him down eventually.

'Don't you think we should reveal all the facts to Kartik and Dipika?' she asked.

'We will, at the right time. Right now, Dipika is very worried about Kartik and he is still struggling to cope. We cannot add to their stress in this situation,' Mihir said.

'But I think ...'

'I said we will. At the right time,' Mihir stated, interrupting her.

He wiped the sweat from his forehead and zoomed away.

~

Kartik's only hope of making everyone believe him was to find the stalker. He was determined to track him down. For an entire week, he went to Cyber Hub every day during office hours to keep watch. It was only a matter of time before he spotted him again, Kartik thought, as he clearly remembered that the man was carrying an office bag. He further connected the dots and concluded that if he worked in one of the companies that had their office at Cyber Hub, he would have to park his bike in one of the three allocated parking lots for two-wheelers. Each of these parking areas faced an exit gate, and he was planning to keep an eye on them. He was playing blind, but he felt his cards were strong this time. There were many black Bullets parked in each of the area lots. He spoke to the security guards, giving them a physical description of the person he was looking for, but none of them had noticed him.

Kartik didn't lose heart. Every day he waited till late in the evening, until all the bikes moved out of the parking lots. But there was no sign of the stalker. On some days, he even waited till the exact time he had seen him on that day. He hadn't told anyone what he was up to, as he didn't want to look foolish again. Somehow, he persisted, and on the eighth day, his efforts were finally rewarded. When office hours were over and he sensed the guy wouldn't show, he walked into the local bar where he had gone on the day he had learnt of Ruhi's affair. After a couple of hours, and a couple of bottles of beer, he walked out, still in his senses. At that moment, he got a call from Tushar.

'Kartik, where are you? Dipika called to tell me that you aren't home yet. She's been trying to call you,' Tushar said. He feared that Kartik was on the right track to find the stalker.

Under the influence of the alcohol, Kartik told him everything.

'I had told you to keep me informed about your activities,' Tushar reacted fiercely. 'Why did you have to do all that alone? Please go home right away and we will chalk out a plan tomorrow. This isn't the way to track someone down. People may file complaints, if they feel you are stalking them every day.'

'I wish I had filed one; I wouldn't have been here today if I had,' Kartik said and sighed. He disconnected the call, started driving, and took a left on the highway. Right at that moment, he saw the rider again—the same black Bullet and helmet.

*The stalker, it's him. This time, I'm not going to spare him.*

Kartik neither honked nor shouted this time; he wanted to follow him and find out where he lived. He drove behind him, keeping a safe distance of at least two metres between them to stay out of his sight. Despite two bottles of beer, his senses were alert. He wasn't hallucinating; this was finally happening for real. If Kartik had a gun, he could have shot him dead. Such was the anger inside him. But he kept his cool, though his blood was boiling. Suddenly, the bike stopped by the side of the road. Kartik too came to a halt, a considerable distance behind. He saw the stalker taking his phone out of his pocket and removing his helmet.

*The same long hair. It's him. I will not let him win this cat-and-mouse game this time.*

How badly Kartik wished to get out of his car and drag him off his bike by his collar. But he didn't want to lose him again by acting impulsively. He waited patiently as the rider made his call.

*Who are you, and why did you kill Ruhi? Whoever you are, I am going to beat the brains out of you. You have made me go crazy, to the extent that I started hating myself. But not anymore; I'll prove to everyone that you are the culprit. I'll expose you, and you'll be left with absolutely nothing. You are just hours away from your end.*

~

'Didn't I tell you not to stay in the city for longer than a week? Why are you behaving like a mutton-head?' Tushar yelled as soon as Shishir picked up the call.

'Today is my last day. You don't know how difficult it was for me to convince them to transfer me back. I had to lie and tell them that my mom's health is critical and she needs me. You think that was a cakewalk?' Shishir retaliated with equal aggression this time.

'Whatever. Kartik is on the lookout for you near Cyber Hub. Pack your bags and leave tonight. I am saying this for your own good.' Tushar said. He told him what Kartik had said to him.

'I need to talk to you before I leave. All this is getting on my nerves. I feel like a criminal. It was just a mistake.'

'Come home, but you have to leave tonight.'

'All right.' Shishir disconnected the call, put on his helmet, and sped off.

~

As soon as the bike started moving, Kartik began following it again. He didn't let his focus waver even though a million thoughts were flashing through his mind. He knew he was finally about to decode the mystery of Ruhi's murder. After a few minutes, the stalker took a familiar route. Kartik was a little surprised, but he made sure that he stayed out of sight. After a few more turns, the biker entered a lane. Kartik's blood ran cold. *Please, not the last apartment on the lane; anywhere but there*, Kartik muttered under his breath. But that was exactly where he parked the bike. Seeing the stalker enter Tushar's apartment, Kartik was horrified and could no longer comprehend what was going on. Kartik stared at the bike and the apartment's entrance in disbelief.

*This is unreal. Why has the stalker gone into Tushar's house? Do they know each other? And if he does, why wouldn't he believe my statements? Was he involved too?*

*And does Dipika know about any of this? This is unreal …
this is really bad. Fuck, this is unbelievable.*

Kartik wanted to break the door open, walk into
Tushar's house and ask him what the hell was happening.
But he decided to wait. After a few minutes, the stalker
came back outside again. Kartik could see him clearly
now. There was no doubt that he was the person with
whom Ruhi had been arguing that evening. And he
felt in his gut that it was he who had broken into their
house that same night.

Once the man had left on his bike, Kartik walked up
to the entrance of Tushar's apartment and banged on
the door while ringing the bell furiously. Tushar opened
the door, looking rather alarmed. Without greeting him,
Kartik strode in and took a seat. For a while, he kept his
eyes on the floor and took deep breaths.

'Are you okay? What are you doing here at this
time?' Tushar asked, giving him a glass of water. There
was another glass on the table beside him. The stalker
drank from it, Kartik thought. He wanted to smash it
to the ground, but he managed to restrain himself and
spoke coolly.

'I must ask you this. What was the stalker doing
here at this time of the night? I need an explanation
from you.'

'Stalker? And here? You are mistaken, Kartik. Okay
… wait a minute, are you drunk again?' Tushar leaned
over as if to smell the alcohol on Kartik's breath.

Kartik pushed him away lightly, saying, 'Never mind
that; I am in my senses. I told you, I was at Cyber

Hub. I saw him there tonight and followed him here. Minutes ago, he entered your house. Why the fuck are you behaving as if you don't know anything? Were you also involved in Ruhi's murder? Have you been trying to manipulate us all this time?'

'You've got to be kidding me. The person who had just come was no stalker. He was my friend, Shishir. He returned to Gurgaon recently and dropped in to see me after office hours.'

'He isn't just your friend. He is a stalker. The one I've been talking about all these months. He is a murderer.' Kartik had begun yelling.

'Okay, calm down,' Tushar said, trying to pacify him. 'Are you sure Shishir is the man you saw outside your house?'

'Yes, I am bloody sure,' Kartik responded firmly. 'You ought to give me his address right now.'

'Give me some time. Let me talk to him first,' Tushar requested, as if he were trying to bring the situation under control somehow.

'It's not the time to talk now. I want his address before he disappears again. Right now. Please Tushar, don't make this complicated. I don't know what you are up to, but I want to close this chapter tonight, once and for all.' Kartik took a deep breath to steady his heartbeat.

Seeing that he had no option but to comply, Tushar messaged him the address on his phone. Without waiting another minute, Kartik left, slamming the door behind him. Tushar immediately called Dipika and told her what had happened, leaving his involvement out of it.

Kartik had decided to go for it; it was now or never, as he didn't want to give Shishir time to escape. En route to the address Tushar had given him, he called Mihir to inform him that he had found Ruhi's stalker and was on his way to his house.

'If you're sure that he is the stalker, then please wait … I don't want you to go alone. I'll join you. What's the address?' Mihir asked, as he got out of bed to change. He didn't want Kartik to get hurt.

'The address is only a few kilometres away from your house. It'll take time for me to reach; these bloody trucks have jammed the highway as usual. But you get ready by then. I'll pick you up on the way.' Kartik was driving with his phone on speaker mode.

'No, go straight to the address. I'll be there. Wait for me,' Mihir said, and disconnected the call.

Kartik was stuck in heavy traffic; his car was hardly moving now. He checked his phone. Dipika had called several times. He didn't want to pick up because he knew Tushar would have spoken to her. Right now, he didn't want to fall for any emotional blackmail. She had sent a message as well. He opened it and read:

*Kartik, you are behaving abnormally. Tushar has told me everything. You are drunk and I request you not to drive around in this state. It isn't safe and it's against the law too. Please come back home; Tushar has promised to talk with that friend of his tomorrow. We will sort it out.*

Kartik decided not to reply. As soon as the traffic cleared, he entered the sector mentioned in the address and somehow managed to find the exact location. He parked the car on a lane behind the house and looked around for Mihir. There was no sign of him. He called him, asking where he was, to which Mihir replied that he would reach in a few minutes. Dipika kept calling, but he didn't pick up.

By now Kartik was impatient to go inside; the lights were on. He had already waited long enough for Mihir, he decided. He rang the doorbell several times, but no one opened the door. He was sure the person inside was avoiding him. He looked around and noticed that one of the windows was open and didn't have a grille. Putting his phone on silent mode, he climbed in through the window. Once inside, he stood listening for sounds of activity, his heart was pounding. He could hear the ceiling fan from one of the bedrooms. In all probability, the stalker was alone in the house, he concluded. He couldn't have asked for a better opportunity than this. Kartik was nervous as hell, but he was determined to beat the shit out of him. He wanted to ask him what had made him kill Ruhi, and force an answer from him. All these months, no one had known the truth of what happened that night. Now he was moments away from unravelling the mystery. Images of Ruhi lying dead on the floor flashed in front of his eyes. He walked slowly towards the bedroom, almost holding his breath. He entered the room softly and looked around.

There he was, sitting at his study table, dead.

Kartik froze at the scene. There was blood all over the man's shirt; his eyes were still wide open. Someone had stabbed him.

Kartik gazed at him, thinking how desperately he had wanted to prove his existence for months. He couldn't comprehend what he was witnessing; his head spun with disbelief. As he took a couple of steps back, he could feel the numbness in his legs. As he was backing out of the room, he spotted a book on the expensive study table which had a flashy cover. It looked like a personal diary. Kartik picked it up, hurried out of the room, and exited from the same window through which he had entered. As he ran towards his car, he crashed into Mihir who had just arrived.

Mihir could see the fear on Kartik's face. Never before had he seen him so frightened.

'Are you okay? What happened?' Mihir asked, holding him by his shoulders.

'Run ... run ...' Kartik gasped. 'He's dead.'

## chapter thirteen

'Run ... run ...' Kartik had said. But where do you run when you're being chased by your own soul? It felt like he was standing in front of distorted mirrors, viewing versions of himself that he hadn't seen before; the more he tried to run away, the more he ran into them. Would he ever find a way to reach the exit? Suffocating, drowning, adrift in the maze of his own mind, every twist and turn took him deeper into the darkness. The more he tried to solve the maze and reach the other end, the more he was pushed into this never-ending game. The stalker was dead; the face that had haunted him for months had turned cold and stiff. That should have satisfied Kartik; he had wished him dead all these months. Now he just wanted to run as far and as fast as he could, hoping no one had seen him.

Kartik and Mihir drove their cars as fast as they could out of the lane, stopped near Mihir's house and got out. Kartik was still in a state of shock.

'I told you to wait for me. What the fuck happened?' Mihir looked panicked.

'He's dead. It's Tushar, he is behind all this. The stalker was at Tushar's home earlier ... he has been protecting him all these months.' Kartik was still breathing heavily. 'In his room ... his bags were packed, which means he was about to escape once again. And Tushar was trying to manipulate me to wait for a day or two, to prove yet again that the stalker doesn't exist ... and all of it was simply my drunken hallucination ...'

'Have you gone nuts? Why would Tushar ... fuck, I can't believe this.'

'Now I realise why he wanted me to update him on all my activities after I told him that I'd seen the stalker again,' Kartik continued.

'But how's he related to Tushar, and what's his motive for doing all this?'

'Only Tushar can answer this. We have to go to Tushar's house right now before he gets to know that the stalker is dead,' Kartik concluded, and was about to get back into his car when Mihir stopped him.

'You're drunk. I'll drive.' He took the keys from Kartik and got into the driver's seat.

*Who should I trust? What are the parameters of trustworthiness? I trusted Tushar, how could I not trust him? He's my sister's boyfriend, but what made him save my other sister's killer? My mind's screaming that he was also involved somehow, but my soul disagrees. Whom should I really trust?*

The winds of doubt were tearing every withered leaf from the tree of Kartik's heart.

They hardly spoke on the way. It didn't take long to reach Tushar's house at that hour. As soon as Mihir had parked the car, Kartik rushed to the door and rang the bell urgently. When no one opened the door after a few minutes of continuous ringing and knocking, his eyes fell on the door lock.

'The house is locked,' he said, turning to Mihir. Then he called Tushar on his phone. It kept ringing, but no one picked up even after multiple attempts.

'Damn it.' Kartik kicked the door in frustration.

Mihir still had a puzzled look on his face. He was finding it difficult to comprehend what was happening. Till a day before, he hadn't believed that Ruhi's stalker even existed. Now he was dead. And he happened to be friends with Tushar who was currently avoiding Kartik's calls.

'I think we should leave; there's no point waiting here. Before more trouble comes our way, let's make a move,' Mihir suggested.

Kartik agreed and they drove back to where they had parked Mihir's car. Leaning against the car, they opened the diary Kartik had found on the study table.

*Shishir.* The first page had his name on it. As Kartik flipped through the pages, his heart pounded with anxiety. The diary was now his last hope, the only way to unlock the mystery of Ruhi's death. Mihir was peeping over Kartik's shoulder at the pages while also keeping a watch on their surroundings to ensure they were not being observed.

The diary told them that he worked as a manager at a café in Cyber Hub, and then it struck Kartik why he had never seen him leaving Cyber Hub during regular office hours. After skimming through a few pages, he found what he was looking for—a page with RUHI written in bold letters across the top.

*I was so unprepared for the love that would fill my heart. But there you were with Tushar and Dipika in my café. I wish Tushar had told me that he was bringing such a gorgeous girl along with his girlfriend, I would have arranged something special. I had no idea what this love would feel like, for I had never experienced it before. Where once lay emptiness and despair, there was now a spring of hope. Suddenly, I felt as if my heart would explode. My heart demanded that I make you mine, but I wasn't even able to approach you. I didn't have the guts. I have never felt this way about a girl, and that's what makes me nervous. But I want to be friends with you, to know you and to be with you. I want to see you smile; I don't know why, but there is a strange attraction that I am feeling. It's like the home run feeling, a feeling of jumping over a fence. I was swept off my feet the instant my eyes fell on you! And when you winked at me after you placed your order, I felt like I couldn't breathe. I know nothing about your life, but I love you, Ruhi; I have loved you since the very first moment I saw you. I don't expect the same from you; you're beyond my reach, I know.*

Kartik glanced at Mihir as he turned the page. He looked hurt and disturbed. Pooja was calling him, but he disconnected the call, impatient to read more. Did Ruhi really have an affair, Kartik wondered, as he flipped through a few more pages until he found another passage.

*You're going to have me by your side, whether you like it or not. I'm not going to let go. I will be patient. I will understand that you need your own personal space. And don't worry, I won't intrude on it. I've met a lot of people in my life who have had an impact on me. I've learned different things from everyone. Life lessons, jokes, a whole range of insights. Yet, there's one person who I can honestly say has changed my life forever. And that's you. Many times after that day, Tushar and Dipika have visited my café. But you never accompanied them. Was it because of me? Was my attraction so obvious that you never returned? But my feelings aren't fake; trust me, they are genuine. I am waiting for you ... to meet you, to hold you, to make love to you.*

Kartik was tempted more than once to throw the diary away; reading Shishir's words angered and frustrated him. Mihir was silent throughout, not knowing how to react. But the need to know what had happened made them persist.

*Today, you came again. I was pretty tired after working at the café all day long, but your visit brought a big shining smile to my face. I didn't even care if we would actually hook up; I was just happy that you were there. You are a complete stranger and yet so familiar; it feels like you have always been in my heart. But today, you came with a guy;*

*at first I thought he was your friend. I realised after a while that he is more than that. He's your boyfriend. That hurt me terribly. Knowing that you are already with someone else shattered me. I could not even bring myself to look at the two of you together, but finally I convinced myself that it's your life and you should decide who you want to be with. Anyway, I barely exist in your life. Maybe this was the shortest love story ever. I won't get in your way; I am not the kind of selfish person who would spoil a relationship on purpose. I'll always be your well-wisher from a distance. Your happiness is all I want. Maybe, one day, I'll find a better girl, but I fear I'll only picture you in her.*

Kartik's anger reduced a little and confusion took over. Was Shishir really the culprit? It was hard to say at this point, but one thing was evident. Ruhi didn't have an affair with him.

'Do you still think she had an affair?' Kartik asked with moist eyes.

Mihir sighed; he was speechless.

Kartik added, 'I told you she was hiding something and no one believed me. Not even you.'

Kartik skimmed over a few more pages and started reading again.

*I was almost over you. It had been months since you visited the café. But yesterday, when you came in, you were disturbed. Your boyfriend hadn't accompanied you; you were all alone, arguing with someone on the phone. I assume it was your boyfriend. Is he hurting you? It looks to me like you aren't happy with him anymore, though all seemed well between you guys a few months ago. I could see tears in your eyes, and I wanted to wipe them away, but I knew I had no right to. All I could do was give you a complimentary pastry to lighten up your mood. You smiled at my gesture, but there was pain hidden behind your smile this time. If I were in his place, I would never let you cry alone. But who am I to think all this? Just your well-wisher; not even your friend. But I promise that I will ease your pain in any way I can. Without even letting you know, I will find the reason for your tears. And if it turns out to be serious, I will approach you only to help you. If I can be of any help, I will be really glad. But I also hope that I am wrong, that your sorrow will pass, because all I want is your happiness. In the end, you simply have to trust me. Believe that I won't hurt you like he does. I'll not break your trust like he does. I care for you genuinely, and will never ever do something that'll break your heart.*

Kartik couldn't speak. Mihir, too, seemed shocked as he stood frozen beside him. Silence filled the air as Kartik closed the diary after a minute, considering how wrong he had been about Shishir the whole time.

Mihir was getting continuous calls from Pooja, and eventually he picked up. He narrated briefly what was happening, concluding that it looked like Shishir hadn't had an affair with Ruhi after all. In all probability, he hadn't killed her. Pooja was shocked to hear this and wanted him to explain, but Mihir said he would call her later and hung up. She instantly messaged him:

*If he didn't kill her, then who is behind it?*

Neither Mihir nor Kartik had an answer to that. The one who knew the truth was no more. Kartik opened the diary again, and flipped through a few more pages. But to his utter dismay, several pages had been ripped out of the last section of the diary. Somebody had intentionally torn the pages so as not to reveal what was written in them.

*No, no, this is not happening. It can't get this ugly. It means this was planned. Shit, I am losing it now, I was almost there. Why the fuck does every turn lead to a dead end. I can't take it anymore.*

Kartik was sure by now that Tushar had a hand in this. The only thing he couldn't understand was why he would do it in the first place. He tried to call him but no one picked up. Mihir tried too, with the same result. Panic consumed Kartik's fragile mind, and anxiety shook his exhausted body; he felt tremendous emotions burning inside him. With Shishir gone, the diary had been his only hope. And now, with the torn pages, his hopes too were ripped out!

~

'Do you think your life is a joke? Or am I a joke for you? I've been calling you all night to ask where you are, dying of anxiety, and you don't have the courtesy to even pick up the phone? Not even once?' Dipika blasted Kartik as soon as he came home. By the time he reached, it was early morning.

Dipika had been worried as Tushar had informed her the previous night that someone had killed his friend Shishir, and he had to be at the crime scene in his professional capacity. He had also said that an angry Kartik had taken Shishir's address from him the same night. However, he promised that he wouldn't reveal this information to his colleagues.

'I am not in a state to discuss the number of times you called. The stalker is dead and he happened to be Tushar's friend. His name was Shishir. Your boyfriend was protecting him all these months, pretending that he didn't exist. Here's the diary of the stalker with half of its pages torn out. I am sure Tushar had a hand in it,' Kartik retaliated, showing her the diary. He was still cursing himself for getting to Shishir too late.

'You have totally lost it. Tushar told me everything. If he had revealed that you had gone to that person's house, you would have been behind bars by now. You should thank him instead of coming up with these baseless allegations,' Dipika said forcefully.

'I should thank him? For what? For screwing up my life and for being the reason I had to be in the hospital for seven months? For making sure no one believed my story? Or for manipulating all the facts related to the case and hiding his friend even from his own colleagues on the force? He has been ignoring my calls ever since I found Shishir. Probably if I had the rest of the pages, he would've been exposed by now.' Kartik was furious that Dipika was taking Tushar's side.

'I don't know what your problem is. Instead of understanding the situation, you are sitting here arguing with me. Do you even know what could have happened because of your silly aggressive behaviour? I have had enough of it; I don't want you to make a bigger mess than you already have. I care for you as your elder sister, and I don't know what you're going to achieve by this madness ... but at this stage of my life, I can't afford to lose you again.' Dipika was desperate. Tears rolled down her cheeks at the mere thought of Kartik getting arrested. No doubt the police would eventually release him on discovering that he wasn't involved in Shishir's murder, but she wasn't ready to bear the trauma of waiting for his release all over again.

'I am done with this discussion. If you don't want to support me, it's fine. But I won't spare the person who killed Ruhi. I don't care if he is your boyfriend.' Kartik got up to go to his room. 'You have changed a lot. I didn't expect you to take his side at this stage. I don't know if you knew about all this from the beginning ... but if you had the slightest clue and you still preferred to stay quiet, then I am sorry but I won't be able to stay with you henceforth. You may believe in forgiveness; I don't.' Kartik walked out of the room.

The words penetrated her heart like a sword; he had blamed her too, and that broke her heart. She hadn't expected her brother to accuse her of being involved in hiding the truth. It can't get worse than this, she thought. Just when she believed she had hit rock-bottom, the ground had opened up and swallowed her again. It was as if Kartik's words had dug her grave. She couldn't understand why he was ruining his present and future; she wanted justice for Ruhi, but not at the cost of losing another sibling. She felt robbed, like someone had stolen all her energy and love. She sat there crying, feeling more lonely than ever before. All the days when they had lived together as a happy family flashed in front of her eyes.

*Why can't I smile like before? I watch over you and criticise your actions because I don't want you to suffer more. But the more I try to protect you, the more vulnerable you become and the more helpless I feel. I'm tired, so tired of worrying about you; all it brings is sadness. When will our lives go back to normal? It was all supposed to be over, but it keeps haunting us, and we can't do anything about it. Sometimes, it feels like you're my worst weakness.*

No matter how hard she tried, she couldn't stop her tears. They'd had fights and arguments before, but this had shattered her like nothing else. It was not often that she missed her dad, but today she did. Although he was never as vocal and involved in her daily life as her mom had been, his strong presence had once been soothing. She was realising now that she valued his presence in her life. She picked up her phone and searched among her contacts. He wasn't even in her recent call list; that summed up their relationship these days. But today she felt like she needed him; after much reflection, she dialled his number. He picked up on the first ring.

'Hello, Dad … how are you?' she asked, trying to control her sobs.

Her father immediately realised that Dipika was in some sort of trouble. He had always wanted his children to be close to him, but they had chosen to be distant because of their stepmother.

'Are you okay? Why are you crying? Do you want me to come there?' His concern was reflected in his voice.

'After so many years, Dad, I think it is time to tell you how I feel. I have been putting this off for a long time. I don't want to hurt you through my words, but it is time someone said something and we all know that you're unlikely to be the one to start this conversation.'

'Please tell me, you are my daughter ... your words won't hurt me. But are you okay? Should I come over? We can talk there,' her dad said.

'I am fine, Dad,' Dipika lied. 'We were teenagers, just kids, when you decided to throw us out. We haven't had much of a relationship since then. Do you know how much has changed in all these years? Do you realise how much we've missed your presence?'

'I am sorry, but I always loved you. I wanted you to stay with me.' His voice softened.

Dipika took a deep breath and wiped her tears. 'For years, I waited for you to step up and be a father. All you needed to do was make a simple phone call on a regular basis. The thing is, if you did that, we would've nothing to talk about right now.'

'I did try, Dipika. But Kartik and Ruhi didn't want me around. What was I supposed to do?' Her dad sighed.

'No, Dad, it wasn't us that made the choice. You had the opportunity to choose your priorities. But you chose your married life over your children. Yes, you supported us financially, kept yourself informed about our whereabouts and progress ... but that wasn't enough. As your daughter, it wasn't my job to try to foster this relationship. Still, I tried. But you always seemed less than interested ... except for your formal responsibilities. Would you keep trying to make a relationship work if the other person showed no genuine interest in your life? No, you wouldn't. You never asked me about my relationships, about my work or my dreams.' Dipika recalled all the years during which he had been absent from their lives.

'You are getting me wrong, beta,' her dad tried to interrupt, but Dipika wouldn't allow him to speak; she just wanted to pour her heart out. It had taken her years to be able to say this; every word she uttered had layers of pain hidden in it.

'No, Dad, you can't makes excuses. The situation would have been different if you had lived in another state or country, but you were hardly a few kilometres away. Yet, you chose not to see us often. Maybe our egos kept us apart; we were blaming each other too much. But I wish we had some sort of relationship, I truly do. I've had to grow up watching my friends' close and loving relationships with their fathers. It was strange and heart-breaking to know that I would never have that. I knew that even if we managed to repair our relationship, it would happen when I am much older. Not when I needed you the most during my growing years.'

There was an awkward silence on both ends for some time before her dad spoke.

'I blamed myself for years. I've shed so many tears because I thought I wasn't good enough for you all. I kept trying to do things that would make you proud, things that would make you love me, things that would make you reach out. No father should have to feel this way.'

Dipika replied, 'No daughter should have to feel this way either, Dad. I know you love me, but you don't show it often. Sometimes I would just like to be told that you do. I know that it isn't on top of your list of priorities, but sometimes I wish it was. I know you are not happy, that you have never been genuinely happy with the way things turned out. But the truth is that only you could have changed that. Even now it's not too late. You have to decide once and for all.'

Dipika tried to compose herself, feeling a little relieved at having released a burden she had carried for years. She rubbed her face and eyes to ease the tension and added, 'In your absence, I was forced to behave like an adult, though I wasn't one. I had to care for both Ruhi and Kartik. But I was no expert at raising two teenagers, and sometimes I made mistakes. I tried so hard; I actually thought that if I could make you proud, you would stick around. Age, however, has taught me that pleasing people won't make them stay. I want you to stick around because you want to, not because we want it. Think about it, Dad.'

She hung up, still incredulous that she had actually vented all the frustration that had built up over the years. She was just saying what needed to be said. She wasn't trying to hurt her father, but if she had, then it was because we sometimes hurt those whom we love.

## chapter fourteen

Words hurt, and if they are uttered by the ones you love deeply, they hurt even more. Sometimes, you say something that you don't really mean to someone you love, but by the time you realise it, the damage is already done. Kartik had realised he shouldn't have spoken to Dipika the way he had. She too had emotions, he reminded himself, though she was not in the habit of wearing them on her sleeve. Kartik decided to give her time to recover from the hurt his words had caused. Before he left to meet Tushar, however, he sent her an apology message.

*I know our minds are troubled; you are right from your point of view, but I am not wrong either. I am sorry for what I said; I really mean it. I promise I won't hurt you again, but I want you to understand me and be my strength. I love you.*

On his way to Tushar's home that evening, Kartik had weird thoughts; his mind sought answers to each of the doubts that haunted him. It wasn't easy for him to pursue them all alone, but he was determined to do so. He knew Ruhi's soul would be troubled, and he was ready to do everything in his power to ensure that her soul rested in peace. Earlier, he couldn't bear to see her shed a single tear; how was he expected to endure her death? She had to leave this world before her time, and he was not ready to show any mercy towards the one who had made her suffer.

This time, when he rang the bell, Tushar was quick to open the door. He was expecting Kartik and had already decided how he was going to react. He asked him to come inside and take a seat, but Kartik came straight to the point.

'I need answers. You just can't escape so easily, and if you thought being in the police force would protect you, then you are wrong.'

'You need to calm down.' Tushar took a chair and sat down opposite Kartik.

'No, I won't. Who was Shishir and why were you protecting him? Were you also involved in killing Ruhi? You have been ignoring my calls since last night.'

'Shishir didn't kill Ruhi,' Tushar said in a tone that was intended to put a full stop to Kartik's doubts and suspicions. But Kartik wasn't going to settle for that, and Tushar knew it. So he continued, 'Shishir was my friend, my close friend, in fact. He used to work in a café at Cyber Hub for a long time; it was there that he met Ruhi for the first time. He liked her, but had no hopes of taking it forward—not because she had a boyfriend but because he had his own set of problems. His mom has cancer and is under treatment. So relationships and love affairs were out of the question for him for obvious reasons. We were regulars at his café, but he never expressed his strong attraction for Ruhi. I got to know about it only when I happened to read his diary a while back. He had only begun writing in it at the time. But it was all in his mind. You call him a stalker, but he was actually her well-wisher,' Tushar clarified.

'I have read his diary; I want to know your side of it and what your involvement was in the whole affair.' Kartik, still furious, pulled Shishir's diary out of his bag.

'His diary is with you? Oh god, that's why I couldn't find it when I went to the crime scene with my team last night.'

Tushar stepped forward with his hand outstretched, but Kartik moved away, saying, 'You are manipulating the story again. You either reached Shishir's house before I did last night, or you sent someone to kill him and you deliberately put the diary on his study table after ripping half the pages out of it.'

'You think I planned his murder? You're fucking crazy. He was one of my closest friends, and if I was going to do something like that, I wouldn't have protected him for months. I treat his family like my own; I have taken care of his mom countless times when he couldn't take time off from work. He was like my brother. I looked for his diary last night, hoping to find some clues. I didn't know someone had torn pages out of it until you told me just now. I am sure that its someone who wants to hide the truth,' Tushar explained, observing Kartik's reactions carefully.

By this time, Kartik was partially convinced that Tushar might be telling the truth, but one thing still bothered him.

'If he hadn't done anything, why were you hiding him from everyone?'

'I'm sure you remember that evening; you had seen him arguing with Ruhi. He was actually trying to protect her from some kind of trouble which he refused to tell me about. I asked him numerous times, but he kept saying he had promised Ruhi that he wouldn't disclose it to anyone. He wasn't stalking her; they had been friends for a while. And that evening, he had shared a piece of information with her, something that concerned her. That was why he was hovering around your house; he was trying to get a chance to talk to her. After some time, he left. But the next day, when he heard about Ruhi's suicide, he panicked.'

Tushar closed his eyes in grief and fatigue as he recalled all this. 'I don't know what he communicated to Ruhi that night, but we found nothing on your sister's phone; maybe she had already deleted all the messages from Shishir. But your statement implicating him as a stalker would have gotten him in trouble, though he hadn't done anything of the sort. And he was in no condition to fight a court case or risk getting convicted. It not only takes a toll on your mind, it also empties your wallet. And his mother needed him both financially and emotionally.'

Tushar's eyes were moist by now; he was trying hard not to shed tears, thinking about whether Shishir's mother would be able to survive the shock of his death. He drank from a glass of water before continuing. 'I was sure that you wouldn't take your statement back, and so I advised him to move out of the city. I told him I would handle the rest. As hardly anybody knew him, and nobody else had even seen him in the vicinity of your Gurgaon apartment, I thought that would keep him out of harm's way. But all of a sudden, when the café owner made a proposal of partnership, he returned. The fact that the case had been closed also put his mind at rest. Everything was sorted. If only he hadn't returned, he would've been alive today.'

Tushar remembered how Shishir would smile at the mention of Ruhi's name. 'He always wanted Ruhi to be happy, though he had no hopes of getting into a relationship with her. My intentions were good, Kartik. I really hope you accept the fact that Shishir wasn't who you thought he was.'

Kartik looked at him, expressionless. He felt completely hollow, realising he had nothing in hand despite all the risks he had taken.

Before Kartik could say anything, Tushar added, 'The person who tore the pages from his diary also did a factory reset on his phone. But we are trying to recover the backup of his phone if there is any. Once we find him, he won't be spared.'

Tushar sighed. He could see that Kartik was getting restless and looked at his watch. It was eleven o'clock already. 'Anyway, it's late. I think you should head home.'

Dipika must be worried, Kartik realised. He calmed himself down by taking a deep breath and confessed, 'I had a fight with Dipika in the morning.'

'She told me. I think you should apologise and talk to her, help her understand what's going on in your mind. She loves you a lot. And I know even you do. So, sort it out.' Tushar smiled, getting up from his chair.

*I was really wrong about him.*

'Dipika is indeed lucky to have you. Always be with her. And I'm sorry, I shouldn't have doubted you,' Kartik said.

~

When Kartik returned home, he was guilt-ridden. He wanted to have a word with Dipika and tell her how wrong he had been about Tushar. He wanted to tell her that they made a perfect pair, and that he was sorry for all the baseless allegations he had thrown at her that morning. But she was already asleep and he didn't want to disturb her. Her eyes looked swollen; she must have cried the whole day, he thought. He covered her with a blanket, switched on the air-conditioner, and went to his room to try and catch some sleep. But in the end, he spent the entire night wandering restlessly around the house.

Again, he put pressure on his mind to remember exactly what had happened the night Ruhi died. The last drink, someone taking him inside, the words he had spoken: he remembered everything in bits and pieces. He tried to connect the dots with what he could remember, but still had nothing concrete to go on. He had reached stalemate yet again after finding out that Shishir had not killed Ruhi. His stalker theory was no longer valid. If Shishir hadn't killed Ruhi, he wasn't the one who had broken into the house that night. The words that had echoed in his ears for months weren't uttered by Shishir.

*If that person wasn't Shishir, then who was he? Or was it a hallucination after all?* The thoughts pursued him as relentlessly as his own shadow.

Kartik and Dipika were still asleep in the morning when someone thumped loudly on their door. Dipika, half asleep, opened the door. Kartik too was in the living room by then. It was Inspector Kumawat, who had been in charge of the case. They wondered what he was doing there at this hour of the day. It was hardly six in the morning.

'Are you guys okay?' he asked.

Dipika stood in the doorway, still rubbing her eyes.

'Why weren't you opening the door? What's the matter? I have been ringing the bell for the last ten minutes.'

'We were sleeping. I'm sorry ... but what brings you here?'

'We need to talk.' He asked if he could come in and instructed them to sit.

Kartik thought it must be about Shishir; he was nervous that they had found some evidence of him having been at his house that night. He glanced anxiously at Dipika.

'What's wrong? Dipika asked the police inspector, without taking a seat.

'Wait, give me a second.' The inspector took his phone out of his pocket and made a call.

'They're safe and there seem to be no signs of anyone breaking into the house. Seal the crime scene; don't let anyone inside, not even friends or family.'

His words made both Kartik and Dipika nervous. They couldn't understand what he was talking about, and how it was related to their own safety.

'I think the person you were talking about, the stalker … we found him. But he's dead; he was murdered in his own house. He matches the physical description you had provided. His name was Shishir.'

Kartik nodded, pretending it was the first time he was hearing the news. Kartik was very scared, as he knew he had probably been the last person to enter the house before the police sealed it off.

'So, how's it connected to our safety? You think he killed Ruhi?' Dipika murmured, her eyes wide open with anxiety.

'No, he didn't. Actually, I am here to tell you something else. Look, you need to stay strong.' Inspector Kumawat took a deep breath before saying, 'The thing is, yesterday night, someone murdered Tushar as well.

And he has been stabbed by the same knife which was used to kill Shishir.'

Dipika gasped. She stared at the inspector in disbelief. A sudden chill swept through her body. She felt as if everything was in fast-forward while she was motionless. Before she collapsed onto the floor, Kartik had quickly got up and put an arm around her shoulders. The policeman's words had sunk deep into her chest, choking the very breath from her lungs. Her mind raced as she tried to keep up with a world that was spinning out of control. Her throat held back something between a sob and a shout.

*But Tushar was just fine last night. We had a normal conversation yesterday; no, he can't be gone. Not when he promised me he would be there in every phase of my life.*

'What did he say?' She turned to Kartik, teary-eyed and stunned.

It was painful for Kartik to see her like that. Once the first tear broke free, the rest followed in an unbroken stream. All he could do was embrace her, letting the torrent of her tears soak through his shirt. He could feel her clenching her fists, not knowing whether to go mad or to give up hope all together. He could hear her silently screaming, suffocating with each breath she took. He ran his fingers through her hair, time and time again, in an attempt to calm the silent war within her mind. She wanted to see Tushar right away, but Inspector Kumawat wouldn't allow it. He was sorry for her loss, but he had to do his job. He warned them to stay alert.

'So ... if Kartik was right about what happened that night, and it wasn't suicide, then it means that the killer is still out there—and it is possible that he is the one who killed Shishir and Tushar. We haven't found any information yet, but I want you both to be alert. Maybe you can move to your father's house for a few days, for your own safety?' he suggested.

'No, we are not moving anywhere,' Kartik said, looking up at him while trying to control Dipika's grief.

'You are the only ones connected to all the murders. You are in danger. I am just concerned about your safety,' Inspector Kumawat declared before taking his leave. 'As soon as we get some information, I'll update you. Kartik, you may need to come to the police station to verify that Shishir was the person you had mentioned in your statement.'

The news of Tushar's death shattered Dipika completely. She felt lifeless, as if she didn't belong to this world anymore. All the colours seemed to have faded; even at dawn, she felt darkness engulfing her life. She just wanted the sky to embrace her, to leave everything behind. Her soul had been struck by the hammer of truth, breaking her whole existence. She had no expressions on her face; her feelings had died. She checked her phone and found that it had one unread message from Tushar and a few missed calls. She wanted to talk to him so badly; for the rest of her life, she would regret going to sleep early the previous night. The pain was unbearable but still, with trembling hands, she clicked on the message.

*I have cleared everything up with Kartik. He loves you. Throw away your anger, he needs you. And I don't like to see you cry. I want you to smile always, and I promise I'll never let it fade away. Love you always.*

*You can't break your promise. I need you; you were my strength. How will I survive now? I can't afford to lose you, Tushar, please come back. Will you pick up the phone if I call you now? Please do, I need to hear your voice; I need to hear you say 'I love you'. You told me you will never let me cry, but now nothing is left in my life apart from tears. I am losing myself, please don't let that happen. You can't leave me like this. I love you, Tushar. I can't live without you. Please, for my sake, come back.*

Kartik tried to console her, but she was unmanageable. Losing someone so close is always painful, especially when they leave you unexpectedly. Dipika's life had come to a standstill, and she had absolutely no clue what she was supposed to do now. She had been telling Kartik all along to stay away from all of it and move on, but he hadn't. Now they were losing their loved ones, the few who had remained in their lives, and they still had no answers. First Ruhi and now Tushar—the grief was too much for her to handle.

'I know it's difficult, but please stop crying.' Kartik moved forward to wipe her tears with his hand, but she took a step back.

Wiping her face on her own, she said, 'I don't want to talk to you anymore. If you hadn't continued to probe into Ruhi's death, this wouldn't have happened. I lost

Tushar today because of you. You wanted to know the truth; you would stop at nothing. And what have you achieved by digging up graves? What are you going to do with that truth when you lose everyone? Maybe I'll be the next one to die. Then you'll have to live alone with your truth.'

'I am sorry ... I am so sorry ...' Kartik said. She was right, he thought; he felt responsible.

'You're sorry now ... when Tushar has already lost his life? Damn it, you were at both crime scenes minutes before the murders happened. Do you even understand the seriousness of it? If they find out, you will be charged with both crimes till you are proved innocent. Can you imagine the torture we'll have to go through? I have lost my sister, I have lost my love, and now ...' Dipika shivered, her face had turned pale and tears rolled down her cheeks. 'Please go, I don't want to talk to you now. Leave me alone.'

Kartik felt like he was lost in a thick fog; he cried out but no sound would come. He was living a nightmare, racing through never-ending darkness, all alone with his troubled soul. He had lost Ruhi forever, and now he felt he was losing Dipika as well. He remembered the last words he had spoken to Tushar, '*Dipika is indeed lucky to have you. Always be with her. And I'm sorry, I shouldn't have doubted you.*'

But now, they were only words, mere memories and nothing else.

~

*Strange how quickly things change and how easily roles can be reversed. You cannot hide what resides inside you. That demon, your mind, is like a hurricane. I always feared the destruction it would bring. And now, in the aftermath, I have nothing but scars. It's me, your soul, who suffers because of your actions. I had told you that everything would fall into place over time, but no, you still fell prey to your mind and your thoughts that have only weakened you. How easily you get influenced by the demon's voice! You think that he'll save you, but in fact, he is seeking an opportunity to separate you and me in order to clear the way for himself. Yet when you are completely lost, you come and find me. When every inch of your heart is broken, you search for my presence. After all the mental effort you put in, what purpose did it serve? Only misery and dejection followed.*

*I have told you this before: from time to time, I need to give you a reality check, let you know that I exist. I have reminded you that if I restrain you from even thinking, all your efforts will be fruitless. Believe in me, it's for your own good. When everything else seems to vanish, I'll hold your hand and take you to the next level. You may lose everyone you love, but I'll still reorient you and make you smile through your hard times. And now that the strength of your mind has diminished, my power will only rise.*

## chapter fifteen

'I think it's high time you stopped your investigation and let the police do their job,' Mihir said to Kartik. Dipika needed some time alone, and so he had come to Mihir's house. Mihir was also upset by the news of Tushar's death. Looking at the chaos in all their lives, he didn't want things to take an even uglier turn.

'I doubt they'll make any progress in this case. They're going to close this one citing lack of evidence, just like last time.'

'But, right now, you should think of Dipika and nothing else. That's my view; she needs you the most now. And the more you continue probing, the more it'll hurt her.' Mihir sat down beside him and added sadly, 'I know what it feels like to lose the love of your life.'

'I know, but the killer is out there ... how can I live with that?' Kartik said with moist eyes. He couldn't stop his tears.

'I get your point, but I'll say the same thing that Dipika has been saying since day one. We are only losing more loved ones by pursuing this. And we still have nothing to show for our efforts. It'll be good for all of us to move on. Pooja and I have; I want you to at least try. I see that you are stressing yourself out again; your mental health is clearly deteriorating. You may not be able to feel it, but we do.' Mihir handed him a box of tissues.

Kartik knew that Mihir was right. But the voices in his head weren't allowing him to listen. Every time he tried, something or the other would come up and his mind would be in turmoil again. What was he supposed to do? With each passing day, he could sense that his capacity to think and reason under stress was deteriorating, and he felt the same restlessness that he used to feel at the hospital. It certainly wasn't a good sign; doctors had warned him of these symptoms time and time again. He got up from the sofa and asked Mihir for a cigarette; he needed one desperately. Mihir didn't stop him this time, hoping it would help smoke out the thoughts in his head.

'It's in a drawer in my bedroom, along with an ashtray. But make sure you smoke on the balcony. My mom might come home anytime. I'll join you in a bit.'

*Everyone was wrong about Ruhi, she didn't have an affair,* said a voice in Kartik's head. *So was I, to even consider for a moment that it might be true.*

For months, Mihir had wrongly believing that she had betrayed him. *But it wasn't his fault; Ruhi had lied to him. Yet, he loved her so much, he had planned to get engaged anyway,* Kartik thought.

Kartik opened Mihir's drawer and looked for the pack of cigarettes. He couldn't find it and so he rummaged through the drawer. He took out a few papers and empty packs that were cluttering the drawer. What he then saw almost made him lose his balance. There was the gold ring that Mihir had given Ruhi on her birthday a couple of years ago!

*Why is it here? She wouldn't have returned it to Mihir for sure. She was certainly wearing it that night. That's it. I've got my answers.*

He took out the ring with trembling hands and observed it closely; it was hers. Mihir came in from the other room at that exact moment, saying, 'I'm sorry. The pack was in my bag; I thought I'd kept it in the drawer.'

He saw a furious look on Kartik's face and the gold ring in his hand. He squeezed his eyes shut and said, 'I should have kept it in the locker. From the day I saw it inside the drawer, it's been in here.'

'Why the fuck is this with you? Ruhi was wearing it that night. I've got my answers!' Kartik yelled as loud as he could.

'What answers? Yes, it is the ring I gave Ruhi,' Mihir said in a very casual tone.

'Exactly.' Kartik had him by his collar in an instant.

'What are you doing? Please let go of me,' Mihir said, trying to pull away.

'You were lying the whole time. Now I know why you were telling me to move on.' Kartik punched him hard.

Mihir's jaw hurt, but he didn't react with the same aggression. 'Kartik, have you lost it? Ruhi gave it to me that morning. We had met before our evening plans.'

'You're lying again.' Kartik held him by his collar again.

'I'm not. I told you that I planned to give her a diamond ring the next day. She insisted that I should exchange this ring to pay for it; I hadn't saved enough to buy the ring she liked. And she wanted only that one. So she handed this ring over to me in the morning. I didn't have time to exchange it in the afternoon as I had to get all the party stuff you'd asked me to bring. I planned to do it the next morning.'

'It's a lie.' Kartik didn't loosen his grip on him even though he saw tears rolling down Mihir's cheeks.

'If you think I did it, hand me over to the police. I could never imagine hurting her even a little, and you are alleging that I killed her? There are a few things that you have to trust about a friend; I can't prove this to you. Don't jump to the most obvious conclusion. We have already lost too much in this guessing game.' Mihir's teary eyes were pleading with him to believe that he wasn't involved, but Kartik wasn't convinced.

'Shut up,' he said.

'Kartik, I would never hurt her. You talk about facts? If we take that into account, it's a fact that you were the one to pour all of us our last drinks. Later, the police found sedatives in her drink. I never told anyone this, as I know you would never hurt Ruhi. You don't remember; you were totally drunk.'

Kartik pushed him and started walking away. His head was spinning; he was going mad just thinking about it all. Only minutes ago, he thought he might be able to pull through this with his sanity intact. But he hadn't expected this. Mihir tried to stop him as he pushed the front door open. 'Kartik, you are totally wrong.'

'Maybe, but I just don't know what to believe any more.'

He left, slamming the door behind him, but the words Mihir had uttered hammered in his head. He was losing his mental composure rapidly. Were these the signs of his sickness returning? Was he, Kartik himself, the killer he was searching for? He was losing himself again in the search for the truth. The words echoed in his head: *You were the one to pour all of us our last drinks.*

~

Overthinking certainly kills your happiness. Kartik had been looking for that one person who was responsible for Ruhi's death, thinking it would bring him satisfaction. But it only added to his misery. For hours, he wandered on the streets, stressing himself out over Mihir's words.

*If I was the one to pour the last round of drinks, did I mix the sedatives in hers? But why would I do that? Is it possible that she had told me that she was pregnant and I lost my head? Am I already a psycho or am I turning into one?*

He pulled at his hair, trying to recall the events of that night. He wanted to bang his head on a wall just to make the memories come back. However hard he tried, he would only find himself back, over and over again, on the long stretch of lonely unrest that he was walking now. He wanted to run away from himself as the voices in his head yelled that he was the one who served Ruhi her last drink. If it turned out to be true that he had actually killed her…. Catching sight of his reflection in a window, he felt he wanted to smash his own face. Was this the face that his soul wanted him to see?

*I didn't kill her; she was my sister. I loved her.* He kept repeating those words, but the voices in his head wouldn't stop. He saw that Dipika was trying to call him, but he didn't pick up as he was overcome by guilt. He didn't have the courage to face her. He felt it was solely because of his desperation that they had reached a stage in their lives where they couldn't see any path ahead. If he hadn't continued to probe into Ruhi's death, Tushar would still be alive. All along he had believed his subconscious mind was trying to tell him what had actually happened. And now that it was in front of him, he felt the truth was pointing to him as the culprit. After a while, he switched off his phone. If it was in his hands, he would much rather have switched off his life.

~

'I'm sorry to disturb you, but Kartik hasn't come home yet. Are you both still together? We had a fight and now he isn't taking my calls.' Dipika sounded heartbroken as she spoke to Mihir on the phone.

'Is that what happened? He left my place a while ago; he had an argument with me too. I don't know what's wrong with him. Anyway, I'll try calling him. You please take care of yourself.'

'Please let me know if you hear from him. I'll do the same,' Dipika pleaded.

'You don't need to tell me that. I'll let you know right away. Anyway, did they allow you to see Tushar?' Mihir wanted to divert her attention from Kartik.

'Tomorrow. They haven't released his body yet,' Dipika replied with a heavy heart.

On the one hand, Tushar's death had devastated her, and on the other, Kartik's behaviour was making her feel completely helpless. It wasn't the first time that Kartik was behaving like this. But today, she needed him to be strong for her. She was going through a lot, and she wanted someone by her side with whom she could share her grief and express how she felt.

It was late in the evening when Kartik got home. Dipika had been waiting for him since she had called Mihir several hours back. As soon as the doorbell rang, she rushed towards the door. Seeing Kartik there, she was tremendously relieved and was about to say something but he walked past her with his head down and went into his room. She immediately called Mihir and informed him that Kartik was back. Then she followed her brother to his room.

'I'm sorry about before. I shouldn't have blamed you.' She had gathered her composure and was hiding her grief.

Kartik broke down. All his guilt overflowed as he sobbed violently in her arms. He didn't talk but his tears spoke a thousand words.

'I should have been here with you all along ... I don't know ... I think I'm losing myself again and I don't want that to happen. I don't want to go to the hospital again, leaving you alone. I promise, I won't let it happen again,' he cried.

'I know it's a hard time for both of us, but we have to be each other's strength. We just can't keep going over what has happened. I need you as much as you need me.' With those words, Dipika tried to console her own heart as well.

The loss of their loved ones may have created a rift between them, but their love for each other still held them together. Dipika wanted to tell Kartik how much she wanted to meet Tushar one last time. Kartik wanted to tell her that his guilt was driving him insane. He tried to speak up a couple of times, but he had no words; what was he supposed to say? That he was the one who gave Ruhi her last drink? That all these months he had been searching for her killer, and now life had shown him his own face in the mirror? But keeping this guilt inside hurt him more. After struggling with his mind for quite some time, he finally confessed to Dipika when she was in the kitchen making tea for both of them.

'I killed her,' Kartik murmured, standing in the doorway.

Dipika hadn't heard what he said properly. She turned, asking him to repeat what he'd said. She saw the pain in his eyes; he'd never been able to hide anything from her all these years, and now she knew something was terribly wrong just by looking at him.

'I killed her. I was the one who poured the last round of drinks for everyone that night. I remember, it was me,' he repeated in the same tone.

'What? Now where the fuck is this coming from? We just promised to be each other's strength, right?'

'It's the truth. I don't know how and why; I don't remember that but ...'

'Listen, let me just close this once and for all. You haven't done anything. Neither you nor me; we both loved her more than ourselves. And even in our worst nightmares, we couldn't have imagined hurting her. I have faith in you, as much as I have in myself. So, no more foolish theories. You were her brother. Ask your soul ... would you do something like that?'

Kartik fell into her arms wordlessly. His remorse was now gone. He couldn't fathom whether it was because he had released his feelings of guilt through an emotional outburst or because he realised that Dipika trusted him completely. But he felt tremendous relief. Dipika could sense that Kartik was slowly coming back to normal and nothing could have made her happier than that. Indeed, there's no better friend than a sister, and there was no better sister than Dipika.

~

'Where have you been? We were worried about you,' Mihir asked when Dipika opened the door and he walked in with Pooja. After taking a seat next to Kartik in the living room, he added, 'I tried looking for you in all the places you were likely to visit in our neighbourhood.'

'Why don't you try acting in some suspense movie? You give us goosebumps so often in real life that it's too much too handle,' Pooja said, trying to lighten the mood.

'What brings you both here at this time?' Kartik asked curiously.

'Dipika told me you are home and I rushed here. We've been in constant touch since she told me that you're ignoring her calls again.'

'Smartphones are wasted on you; next time, I think we'll try calling you on various landlines,' Pooja teased. She knew the situation was tense, but hoped to see smiles on their faces.

'I'm fine now. You can relax … I'll just change my clothes and be back.'

Kartik went to his room and Pooja accompanied Dipika to the kitchen where she began making coffee for everyone. Kartik checked his mobile phone, which was charging in the bedroom. Among the notifications was one that he couldn't ignore. It was a text message from Inspector Kumawat. It read:

*Don't go anywhere; stay in your house. I'll be there in a few minutes with my team.*

*What does he mean,* Kartik wondered. *Has he found the person who is behind all the murders? Or does he have another piece of news to shatter their lives?* It was only then that Kartik saw his missed calls. Inspector Kumawat had called him numerous times. His first impulse was to tell everyone about this, but he stopped himself, remembering the promise he had made to Dipika just minutes ago. Kartik changed his clothes and looked for his comb in his bag. As he put his hand inside, something sharp cut him. He removed his hand from the bag to see blood on it.

*What's that?* He clenched his fist tightly, trying to stop the blood flow, but it only got worse. Gritting his teeth against the pain, he unzipped the bag completely with his left hand to find a knife inside.

*Damn, this can't be real.* He remembered Inspector Kumawat telling him in the morning that the murder weapon in both cases was a knife. Someone was framing him in the murders of Tushar and Shishir. He took the knife out of the bag and had a closer look. It had been cleaned.

*How did this get inside my bag? I didn't even take it anywhere today. Someone planted it there to frame me.* He looked around the room and ran towards the window to check if someone could have entered through it. But it was locked from inside. He went to the other one; that too was locked. He opened the window, stuck his head outside and groaned. It was anyway impossible for someone to have come up that way. Only a person who was inside the house could have done it. No one apart from Dipika had been there since morning, as far as he knew. Kartik rushed out to the living room where the others were seated, drinking coffee.

'I found this knife inside my bag, someone is framing me,' he said, panting. 'That person also ensured that I would be the last one to visit Shishir and Tushar's houses before the murders were discovered. Now I get it, it was all planned.'

'Why would someone do that?' Dipika got up from the sofa, almost spilling the coffee in panic.

'The windows in my room were locked, and there's hardly any chance that someone entered that way anyway. Did anyone come home after I left? Whoever was here is the culprit.'

'No ... no one whom I would find suspicious,' Dipika replied instantly.

'Please try to remember.' Kartik walked up to her and put his hands on her shoulders. Dipika was stunned. Who could it be, she asked herself. She shook her head once again, confused.

'Anyone, a friend of yours or one of Tushar's colleagues? It could be anyone. It has to be that person!'

Dipika was speechless; for a moment, she felt like someone had pulled the ground out from beneath her feet. She pointed towards Mihir, who looked at her anxiously.

'Only Mihir came over in the afternoon. He was here for some time … and then left to search for you.'

Kartik froze and stared at Dipika with wide-open eyes. Then he turned his piercing gaze on Mihir, who was completely silent. As they locked eyes, it all became clear to him. He picked up a glass bottle that was on a table beside him and threw it at Mihir. He ducked, and it missed his face by mere inches and fell down on the floor.

'What the hell are you doing? I haven't done anything!' Mihir shouted, trying to save himself as Kartik pounced on him fiercely. Kartik was shocked and furious; his head spun as he began to recall all the lies his best friend had told him.

'You were the one who put those sedatives in her drink, you were the one who reached Shishir's place before me, and I am sure it was you who also killed Tushar. I am going to fucking tear your chest apart. Your time's up!' Kartik screamed.

'You think I killed her? That's crazy. You're losing your mind once again. Dipika, please tell him,' Mihir retaliated. Pooja and Dipika were both too stunned to react. They could barely comprehend what was going on or whom to believe. After several pleas for help from Mihir, Dipika came back to her senses to see Kartik sitting on his chest, raining hard blows on him.

'You lied that she had had an affair. You knew from the beginning that it was your child. You cooked up a story to save your ass and made everyone question her character. Didn't you?'

'Kartik, that's really insane. You need to calm down,' Mihir said, trying hard to extricate himself, but Kartik had pinned him to the floor. His face was covered with blood and the sight of it horrified both Dipika and Pooja.

'Now I know why Shishir, that poor guy I believed was Ruhi's stalker, was hovering around that night. He wanted to warn her—about you.'

Mihir pushed Kartik with all his strength and released himself from his grip. 'You have gone nuts,' he said, wiping the blood off his lips.

Quick to regain his balance after reeling back from Mihir's push, Kartik threw the knife he was holding forcefully towards him. It made a cut on Mihir's forearm as he tried to shield himself.

'What the fuck?' he shouted in pain, holding his arm and falling to the floor.

'Kartik, please stop it.' Pooja rushed towards Mihir; he groaned as she knelt beside him. She was utterly traumatised by their actions and began crying loudly. Dipika ran over and tried to restrain Kartik. Somehow, she managed to take out her phone and call Inspector Kumawat.

'I need you here, Inspector. Right now. Kartik is all over Mihir ... and we found the murder weapon.' She still had a firm grip on Kartik, but in the next few minutes, he managed to free himself and pulled Mihir by his hair. As Pooja tried to stop him, he pushed her away. Mihir succeeded in moving away from him and picked up his phone to call an emergency number on his contact list.

'Hello? I need an ambulance in Sector 7, Gurgaon. Kartik, who was a patient in your hospital until a few months ago, has suffered a breakdown again. He has attacked me. Please come soon.'

A sudden silence consumed the air. It was as if he had crossed an endless ocean, not a sea of translucent water but a vast ocean of never-ending blackness, a sea of darkness. Throughout, he had flailed his arms in the air, hoping a passer-by would see and hear him in distress, but no one had. But now it was over. His best friend and Ruhi's boyfriend was the mastermind behind those terrible crimes. The realisation crushed his heart into pieces; she had loved him unconditionally only to be betrayed in every conceivable way.

The knowledge pierced his heart like a knife. In a second, Kartik had advanced. He grabbed Mihir's hair and jerked his head back, holding the knife to his throat.

'Please, leave me,' Mihir pleaded, but Kartik only pressed the edge of the knife to his throat.

'Please, let him go!' Pooja cried. She looked as if she might faint any second.

Dipika heard the doorbell and ran to open it. Outside, sirens blared and Inspector Kumawat yelled, 'Police.' He pointed his gun at Kartik and Mihir.

'Inspector, thank god you're here. Kartik has gone nuts. He is trying to kill me, thinking I am the one behind all the murders.'

'Kartik, throw away the knife. Drop it right now,' Inspector Kumawat ordered.

'Inspector, please save me,' Mihir continued pleading. Pooja had blacked out and was lying on the sofa by then.

'Kartik, let the police take over. Please, for Ruhi's sake, let go of him.' Dipika had fear written all over her face.

'Inspector … he'll kill me,' Mihir howled.

Inspector Kumawat's gun was pointed at Mihir now. 'My team has just informed me that they have got enough evidence to identify the killer. It was smart of you to erase all the data from Shishir's phone, but Tushar had recovered another phone that Shishir used at the time when Ruhi was murdered. We've retrieved the data—and the truth was hiding in it.'

'It's not the truth. Nothing of that sort happened.' Mihir desperately tried to buy time. In a flash, he pushed Kartik away and picked up the knife that fell from his hand.

'Why won't you believe me, Inspector? It wasn't me … I didn't do it,' Mihir screamed, pointing the knife wildly at everyone in the room as he backed away from them.

Kartik stared at Mihir's distorted face. Even after all that had happened, Kartik wasn't ready to accept that it was his best friend who was responsible for the deaths of three people, including his sister. He recalled how they had lived through good and bad times together, like a family. Sometimes, life doesn't turn out the way we expect, and the end isn't the way we want it to be.

'Mihir, drop the knife,' Kartik said, taking a step towards him. Mihir immediately took a step back. He turned and was about to run when a gunshot rang out. Everyone froze in fear; nobody moved even a muscle.

Kartik closed his eyes and the words from his soul echoed in his mind.

*What can be will only come when time sets right the means to seek it out, and for that you need to believe in me. I'll make sure you believe in my power. You have to, because when the strength of the mind diminishes, the power in me only rises.*

## chapter sixteen

Sometimes, in life, it's difficult to decide what's worse: a lie that brings a smile to your face or a truth that bring tears to your eyes. In both cases, you would be badly hurt in the end. All these months, Mihir had masked his real face with a lie. Now that the truth was out in the open, it shattered everyone who knew him, including Pooja, who didn't have the slightest clue of what was happening behind her back. Not in their wildest nightmares could Kartik or Dipika have imagined that Mihir would put an end to Ruhi's life. They'd had arguments and disagreements, but which couple doesn't? As Mihir got away with one crime after another, he had begun to believe that he could live a lie forever. But the truth has ways of catching up with you.

'Don't you dare tell us anything but the truth. Why did you kill her? Which part of your previous statement was the lie and which was the truth?' Inspector Kumawat sat across the table from Mihir in the interrogation room.

'Only the last two years were a lie.' Mihir sighed heavily; he knew it was the end. He looked at Inspector

Kumawat with a blank face and said, 'She wasn't having an affair; I thought she was, when I read the message that I told you about, but she wasn't. Before I could note the number down, she came out of the washroom. The message was sent by Shishir. I got to know about that later. He had actually revealed to Ruhi that I was cheating on her. I was having an affair with Pooja.'

Inspector Kumawat raised his eyebrows. 'You told me that you got into this relationship after her death, didn't you?'

'I lied.'

'Then tell me the damn truth.' Inspector Kumawat banged the table furiously with his hand.

Mihir kept his head down as he spoke. 'As I said before, everything was fine till a couple of years ago. We had revealed our relationship to Kartik and Dipika. We lived almost like a family. But as the months and years passed, our relationship turned dull. The passion I had felt initially, disappeared. We started fighting and arguing so much and so often that love eventually took a backseat. We were irritated with each other most of the time, but we continued to stay together, trying to give the relationship a chance. Pooja was my moral support during this phase and … I didn't realise when I started liking her. Pooja felt the same. But she thought it was wrong, because Ruhi was her best friend. However, I convinced her that Ruhi and I were together just to keep up appearances, and that the relationship was actually over. It was a few months before that night in

November that I finally managed to convince her. But she wanted me to reveal the truth to Ruhi. I agreed, but in the end I just didn't have the heart to tell her. And then, one day, when I finally gathered the courage to tell her, I found out that she was pregnant. And I just couldn't go through with it.'

Mihir paused for a bit, closed his eyes tight, and said, 'That was my child.'

The expression on his face at this point indicated some remorse. He continued, 'We didn't tell anyone that she was pregnant, not even Pooja. But a few days later, Ruhi got to know about my affair with Pooja. Shishir had taken pictures of us to provide proof; she showed them to me, but didn't disclose who she got it from. I knew that someone was giving her information about us. She never revealed his identity and instead started blackmailing me emotionally. Somehow I managed to convince Ruhi to not disclose it to Pooja. I promised to resolve things, but also made Pooja believe that Ruhi was having an affair and was pregnant.'

'So when things went out of control, you planned her murder along with Pooja?'

'No, Pooja had no clue about it. If she had, she would have stopped me. I wish … but I hadn't even planned it. That evening, during the party, Ruhi was pushing me the entire time to reveal everything that had happened to everyone, including Kartik. She was so upset, she was drinking, despite being pregnant. There I was, feeling like a cat on a hot tin roof. Pooja left early. And Ruhi continued with the emotional blackmail. Even at that point, I had no plans of killing her, but slowly, the alcohol started showing its effect, on me as well as on Ruhi. After her last drink, which Kartik had poured, she almost spilled the beans. She began telling him that I was cheating on her, but Kartik wasn't in his senses anymore and couldn't grasp what she was saying. I took her to her room and somehow calmed her down. In fact, I almost got her to agree that we would move on, but after a while, she began arguing again and even got a little violent. I didn't know if it was the effect of the alcohol … I don't know what it was … but I felt the only option I had was to make her sleep. So I added a heavy dose of pills to her drink. My intention was never to kill her. I wasn't aware that such a step under the influence of alcohol would take her life. I just wanted her to sleep, so I could discuss things with her the next day, when both of us were sober. Once she was in bed, asleep, I came outside, took Kartik to his room, and helped him into his bed. It was then that I called Pooja to tell her that Ruhi had agreed to move on.'

'And you said, "I'll be a free bird", to her on the phone.'

'Yes. The next morning, when I heard the news, I was shattered. I could see the sad faces of Dipika, Kartik and Pooja, but I didn't have the guts to tell them what had happened. The police declared that it was a suicide, and even though I felt I should disclose what had happened, I couldn't bring myself to do it. Kartik's stalker story gave me the much-needed cover. The guilt depressed me to an extent that I started keeping my distance from everyone. If the murder had been planned, I would have happily moved on, keeping no contact with either Dipika or Kartik. But that wasn't the case. And my relationship with Pooja suffered; in all these months of being together, we never really got close to each other.' Mihir's eyes were moist as he realised too late that relationships can only be built on trust.

No matter how much times have changed, and mediums of expressing love have changed, the basics of relationships are still the same. If he could have understood this earlier, they would all still be the happy family that they once were.

Inspector Kumawat said, 'Everything went as you wanted, but eventually Kartik bumped into Shishir. You could have confessed then, rather than choosing to manipulate the truth.'

'It wasn't easy for me to see what was happening to Kartik. When he was in the hospital, I was severely depressed. I should have been happy that I was finally with Pooja, but I wasn't. Guilt made me weak, so weak that I could hardly get Ruhi out of my mind, and I couldn't express this to anyone as everyone was grieving. I couldn't even tell Pooja that I was responsible for Ruhi's death. Eventually, when Kartik was discharged, every time I saw him, I kept drowning in remorse. So, I promised myself that I would be there for him as he recovered. He was still my best friend, and what I had done to him and Ruhi was beyond forgiveness. I never believed in karma but when Shishir came back into our lives, it frightened me. Kartik got hold of his address and informed me that he was going to confront him. I knew that I had to reach Shishir's place before Kartik arrived, and so I told him to meet me outside his house. But I got there first. When Shishir saw me at the door, he asked me to come inside not knowing what my intentions were.

'I killed him and did a factory reset on his phone to delete all the evidence he had on me. I found a diary on his study table and quickly flipped through it. I realised that sections of the diary could be used against me in court and hastily ripped out the pages where he had written that I was cheating on Ruhi. Once I had ensured that no evidence had been left behind, I climbed out of the window, leaving it open for Kartik to enter. I watched him go in from a distance and appeared in front of him only when he came outside again, to give him the impression that I had just reached the spot. He didn't suspect me, and I thought that everything would end there, but it didn't. When we met again the next day, Kartik informed me that Tushar was retrieving the backup on another phone that Shishir had.'

'And so you killed Tushar, thinking everyone around you was a fool. The phone was with our team of experts from the police force, not Tushar. And it contained evidence of your affair, photos and messages that were exchanged between Ruhi and Shishir, which indicated that she knew about it and was depressed. It was only a matter of time, once Shishir's body was found, before we nabbed you. Because of you, three innocent people had to die.'

There are two five-letter words that no one can escape from: one is truth and the other is karma. Floating on a silent breeze, as light as breathless cries, the truth was out at last, no longer obscured by lies. Trying desperately to hide the truth, Mihir had taken a path of self-destruction. One cannot circumvent destiny; one can only take a longer path before eventually crossing ways with karma. What goes around, comes around. There were two sides to the story; no, make that three. There was his side, her side, and the truth. Karma isn't a bitch; it is just fair.